John Buckley, John Charles Buckmaster

A Village Politician

The life-story of John Buckley

John Buckley, John Charles Buckmaster

A Village Politician
The life-story of John Buckley

ISBN/EAN: 9783337070380

Printed in Europe, USA, Canada, Australia, Japan

Cover: Foto ©Raphael Reischuk / pixelio.de

More available books at **www.hansebooks.com**

A VILLAGE POLITICIAN THE LIFE-STORY OF JOHN BUCKLEY

EDITED BY J. C. BUCK-MASTER. WITH AN IN-TRODUCTION BY THE RIGHT HON. A. J. MUN-DELLA, M.P.

LONDON: T. FISHER UNWIN
PATERNOSTER SQUARE. MDCCCXCVII

INTRODUCTION.

The following pages are an interesting record of one whom I have known for many years as a practical and active worker in all social and educational effort. Some parts may read like a romance. The changes made in names and places are intended to prevent a too personal identification. My friend's early life was spent among the farmers and farm labourers in the valley of the Chiltern Hills—for whom he still retains a warm sympathy; and his account of their life and character is told in his own way. Later on he was thrown among the artisans of a town who were carried away on the strong torrent of political excitement which set in soon after the passing of the first Reform Bill. The Anti-Corn Law agitation, and the contested elections arising out of it, afforded a safer and wiser opportunity for assisting in the expression of the current and general discontent of which so many to-day remain ignorant. Disowned by his relations, who were chiefly agriculturists, and treated by his companions and friends with scorn and ridicule, he threw himself heart and soul into the Anti-Corn Law agitation, until towards its close he attracted the attention of Lord Morpeth, who advised him to give up politics and turn his attention to the growing cause of public education. This he did with marvellous energy and success; and this was the turning-, and perhaps saving-point of his future life.

The book cannot fail to be of interest to political believers of the past fifty years, and to offer encouragement to young men to assist in the settlement of questions which are now, or hereafter may be, agitating the country, by instructing them in the struggles and political history of the past, which have won for the present generation the rights and liberties they now enjoy. Ideas and prin-ciples which are treated with the scorn and contempt of one age become the faith of the next.

The early life of the author was full of sorrow and trouble. He had to fight his way through difficulties and trials under which most young men would have fallen. But he has now entered the autumn of life in comfort, and with the esteem of many friends. He has been spared to see the harvest and the full recognition of principles to which his humble efforts were early directed, and in which he was sustained in the darkest hours of temptation and difficulty by the earnest conviction that what is just is right.

I shall be glad if a word of commendation from me will be of service in attracting attention to the simple, struggling life of a young reformer, who was not afraid to sow the good seed in the teeth of many a wintry blast.

A. J. MUNDELLA.

A VILLAGE POLITICIAN.

CHAPTER I.

My mother's funeral—I am handed to the care of my
uncle—My school days—Constantly flogged—The
dog-whip lost—Tied to the bedpost—Get loose and
am found tasting something in a bottle—It is said to
be poison—I am measured for my coffin—A night's
horrible agony, expecting death—Religious teaching
—Determine to fire the shop—My sufferings—Sent
back to Claywick.

I JOHN BUCKLEY, put the following
things on record :—

To wit :—On a dark November night, in the
year of our Lord 1822, a weird procession
started, with horn lanterns, from a lone farmhouse to the village churchyard of Claywick.
It was the funeral of my mother. It was the

custom to bury persons dying from small-pox at night. To be left without a mother at the age of two is often worse than being left without a father. The glimmer of the lanterns threw into relief the few dark figures that stood round the grave; the church bell tolled twenty-three, the age of my mother, and in a short time the village was as quiet as the churchyard. The next morning the labourers trudged heavily to their work, and the sun shone brightly through a dormer window on an orphan child as if nothing of any importance had happened.

The home was shortly afterwards broken up, and I was handed over to the care of my widowed grandmother, who was somewhat advanced in years and suffered from rheumatism. My grandmother and the little house-girl, who was also an orphan, and myself, made up the family circle. Every morning and evening there was the reading of the Scriptures, followed by silent prayer. I was early taught to read and learn simple hymns and texts, as " When my father and mother forsake me then the Lord will take me up." In all the troubles and sorrows of the future I never forgot the hymns and texts of my childhood, or my love for my grandmother—it was often my only comfort. At seven years of age I became, like most boys, troublesome and mischievous, and it was thought I required a firmer discipline.

The misery and wretchedness of life now began. I was sent miles away to an uncle at Oxenbridge, who had the reputation of being a firm, religious, God-fearing man. He was shop foreman to a large builder. It was agreed between my father and grandmother that he should receive ten shillings a week, with the understanding that I was to be religiously brought up, well cared for, and educated. If there had been no other children, the promise might have been better kept. The cruelties inflicted on defenceless, motherless children have never been properly written. I was at once sent to the British school, and every Monday morning I carried my penny tied up in the corner of a red pockethandkerchief. I was frequently kept away from school to mind the baby, a duty which had hitherto been done by a girl who was discharged on my arrival.

In a few weeks I became the domestic drudge of the house, rising early to light the fire, sweep or scrub the room, sift cinders, clean knives and boots, run on errands, and fetch water from the town pump. Perhaps this was a useful training—at any rate, it kept me fully occupied. But to be put all day and sometimes two days on a dietary of bread and water, and flogged with a heavy dog-whip, for being a few minutes late from school, or not in time to fetch the dinner beer, or dirtying my pinafore, was more than I cared to suffer, because I knew most of the punishment was unjust and undeserved. Punishments for wrongdoing, if not cruel, are accepted by a child and forgotten, but unjust punishments are never forgotten. I saw other boys playing after school hours—why was I not to play? In summer-time nearly all the boys went to a little mill-stream to bathe. Why was I not allowed to bathe? As a special reward for dragging two fat children four miles along a dusty road on a hot July day, I was permitted for once, as a great treat, to bathe. I looked forward to this day like a prisoner for his liberty, but when it came it brought no pleasure. When I took off my shirt and saw, what I had often seen before, that my body, from the shoulders downwards, was mottled with bruises, from dark purple to a greenish yellow in colour, I felt so ashamed for the other boys to see it, that I made an excuse that the water was too cold, and I put on my shirt and returned home, to be flogged for not saying where I had been. I can truly say that for weeks and months my body was never free from bruises and wheals.

On going to bed I used to count the marks, as far as I could see them, and I remember one Good Friday night I counted thirteen. A double piece of sash-line (often with a knot at the end), such as carpenters use for carrying their tool baskets with, was a common instrument of punishment. Flogging, which at first was looked forward to with great fear and trembling, soon lost its terror, and the most severe punishment failed at last to bring a tear. Almost every flogging was accompanied with the expression of a regret that God didn't take me when He took my mother, and it was only the fear of the brimstone lake that kept me from following her. But what stung me more than floggings and semi-starvation was to be told, at meal times, that I was only kept out of charity, which at that time I believed. The dog-whip (which used to alternate with the basket rope) was kept on a shelf in a dark cupboard with copies of "Zion's Trumpet" and other good books. The lower part of the cupboard was used for storing firewood.

Once I had spilt some of the dinner beer and must be punished, but the whip was nowhere to be found. I was accused of making away with it. My denial was of course a lie prompted by the devil. I *must* know where it was, and I was to be kept without food until it was found. After enduring the suffering of hunger which I hope few have experienced, I said, "I had sold it to a boy for a halfpenny, but I didn't know the boy." The basket cord then did duty for the whip; the one made bruises, the other wheals. I was sent into a bedroom with a lump of bread and a mug of water and tied with a sash-line to a bedpost. By twisting and wriggling about I was able, like the Davenport brothers, to loose myself, but, unlike them, I was unable to put myself back. I amused myself when loose by looking into all the drawers and cupboards that were not locked, when I came across a bottle partly filled with some liquid which, from the taste on the cork, was not unpleasant. At this moment I heard footsteps on the stairs, and in my hurry and fear I spilt some of the contents of the bottle. I was sent downstairs and flogged. After it was over a workman who made coffins came in for a gossip. All my lying and other sins were told to this man, especially my disobedience in getting loose from the bedpost, which God would now punish.

The end had at last come! The liquid which I had sucked from the cork was declared to be a rank poison, and in a short time it would be all over. The coffin man was instructed to measure me for a coffin. He took a rule from his side-pocket, and as he ran it over my body I felt a cold shudder as he called out, " 3 ft. 4 in. by 1 ft. 2 in. across the shoulders, 9 inches deep; three-quarter elm. Ready to-morrow morning."

All the sorrow and suffering of this world had now attained its climax. The apprehended agony of dying before morning no words can describe. I was ordered to bed. I wanted to kiss the baby and ask forgiveness, but this was denied. I went upstairs to a dark, dingy kind of cupboard which contained a little bedstead, and here I was told to prepare for the fire which is never quenched. Surely no other body but myself ever passed through the sorrowful anguish I did on that awful night. The darkness seemed at intervals illumined with flashes of light. I tried to remember all my sins and wickedness. And I wept and prayed as well as I could to be forgiven—to be spared to see my grandmother once more before I died! I thought I did see her, with a tall white cap, sitting on my bedstead. Did I not hear last Sunday that the Lord had made the wicked for the day of evil, and there was no hope? Every time the church clock chimed I thought, " Perhaps that will be my last." I prayed as well as I could, and cried and struggled until at last I fell asleep. I awoke next morning with my lips glued together, my body hot and feverish,

and my eyes bloodshot. But there was another
stab. My uncle and aunt laughed at my
sufferings, and said, jeeringly, that the bottle
contained nothing but dill water, and they said
it was poison to frighten me and make me a
good boy.

Then, as now, the religious instruction of
youth was considered most important, but it
was chiefly confined to the teaching in Sunday
Schools, and my Sundays were fully occupied.
From half-past nine to a quarter to eleven,
Sunday School; from eleven till one, preaching; from half-past two to four, Sunday
school; from six to eight, preaching again.
Occasionally, the Minister would call. He had
observed I was not so attentive to the sermon
as I ought to be. Then there was tea and
a little prayer-meeting, chiefly for my benefit.
If the Lord saw fit to make me, young as I
was, a chosen vessel, the Minister had no objection. These and similar remarks about the
Potter and the clay, mine elect according to
the foreknowledge of God the Father, with
like sentences in all the sermons and prayers,
formed the backbone of my religious instruc-

tion, until at last I believed I could only be a vessel of wrath. When I heard that at the last day millions would be swept with the besom of destruction into the bottomless pit no one seemed surprised; but a placid smile of satisfaction came over the faces of those who were elected. I began to think if you could not be good it was of no use trying, and I began not to care. My life, so far, had been a burden and a sorrow, except the few years I lived with my grandmother, and every day the wish that I had been buried with my mother made my life wretched.

At the back of the house there was a shed in which the lath-rendings were kept, and in my desperation I determined to set fire to the shed, and burn the place down. I took a tinder-box and matches and began to strike a light, but the flint fell among the rendings and was lost. I soon found another, but as the workmen were moving about the intention was given up. The next day a new flint was found in the tinder-box. What had become of the old one? Unless it was found, I must be punished. The whip which I said

I had given to a boy for a halfpenny now made its appearance; it had fallen from the shelf, and was hidden under blocks of fire-wood, and as these were taken away the whip was found, but not a word was said about its discovery. What surprised me was that I was never flogged either at the British school or Sunday School, although flogging at both places was common.

Scantily clothed in winter and always insufficiently fed, the neighbours, who had some idea of my misfortunes, used to pity me, and often give me food. At school I did sums for boys for part of their dinner. All this time I believed, and others believed, I was kept out of charity. The last winter set in with unusual severity. Hungry and cold, day by day I hobbled through the snow and ice for nearly a mile to school, until my hands were so swollen that I was unable to hold a pencil, and my feet were a mass of sores and chilblains so that I could scarcely walk. One morning the wife of a bricklayer took pity on me, and asked me into her house to have a warm. She gave me something to eat,

and bathed my feet in warm milk and water
and bandaged them up with ointment ; and
this she repeated until the sores were healed.
I sat on a little bench in the chimney-corner
and cried with gratitude for her kindness,
which is as fresh in my memory to-day as if
it had happened yesterday. Forty years after
I returned her kindness by helping her to
a small annuity, which she enjoyed many
years.

Towards the close of the year a man came
and preached in the market-place on the
Second Coming of our Lord. He made out,
from all sorts of prophecies and mathematical
calculations, that at a particular minute on
the night of the 31st of December the
Millennium would begin. Everybody would
be kind to everybody ; there would be a reign
for a thousand years of universal peace and
love—no more floggings, no more hunger, no
more long sermons and prayers. We should
all help one another, and love one another
as members of one family, and be happy.
Now this was exactly the state of things I
wanted, and as it was only a few weeks to

the time I could endure my punishment cheerfully. January came and February came, but no Millennium !

One evening in March I was told that they were all sick and tired of keeping me; I was a great trouble, and I must be sent home and help to earn my living. I could read and write fairly well for a boy of ten. I had committed to memory "the chief end of man," of which I had had some experience of the beginning, and the word made effectual to salvation, with Scripture proofs. Nothing in after-life was so great a barrier to my religious belief as was this catechism; it made me sceptical.

Some time after I was told by my grandmother that my father had been gradually getting rid of his little property, and that he could no longer afford to keep me, and I must come home to work. I was put on board one of Pickford's boats, and arrived at Claywick lock just as the labourers were going to work. I made my way to my grandmother's, who was ready to receive me with a good breakfast. She shed tears over me and kissed me, and these were the first lips that touched my cheek since I left her nearly four years ago. The industry of Cain was now to be my occupation.

CHAPTER II.

CLAYWICK was pleasantly situated in the
valley of a range of chalk hills, partly
covered with beeches, which were used for
making chairs, bowls, and trenchers. The
village consisted of one street with a stagnant
pond in the centre. The parish contained three
large farms and four small ones. The farm-
houses and most of the cottages had an oven,
and a garden fairly stocked with fruit trees.
Outside the village damson-trees grew on the
sides of the road and lanes. The soil con-

sisted of the stickiest and heaviest clay, un-
drained, and in winter the water stagnated
half-way up the furrows, and much of the
autumn-sown wheat perished.

The small farms once belonged to the
ancestors of the families that occupied them,
but they were gradually absorbed to increase
the estate of a neighbouring proprietor. The
houses and outbuildings were now fast falling
into ruin, and when the occupiers died or left
no one succeeded them. I can remember
one or two of them. They rose early, worked
with their labourers, and, until age prevented,
led them in the hay-field and harvest-field,
loaded carts, built ricks, held ploughs, sowed
their corn broadcast, thrashed it with a flail,
and winnowed it with a fan. This varied
work had its pleasurable side. If the farmer
and his labourers could only have lived by it
it would have been a happy life, but there can
be no happiness in a constant struggle for
mere existence.

The wages of the labourers were nine and
sometimes ten shillings a week, and bread
was a shilling a loaf. The weekly wages of

the farm labourer at that time were equal
to one bushel and a quarter of wheat; they
are now equal to three bushels. At hay-time
and harvest-time the labourers were fed by the
farmers; but this only lasted for seven or, at
most, eight weeks in the year, when their hours
were from daylight to dark. Their families
could glean in harvest-time, and skim milk,
butter-milk, and small beer could be had for
asking. The labourers' cottages looked pic-
turesque from the outside, but inside you had a
broken floor. The bricks had worn through and
disappeared, until at last you had little more
than an earthen floor; and when the cottage
tumbled to pieces it was never rebuilt. The
rent was one-and-sixpence or two shillings a
week. The furniture usually consisted of an
oak table, two or three wooden chairs, an oak
chest, a stool or settle, a dough cover, an
earthenware pan for water, and a Dutch clock.
The fire was on the hearth, and an iron pot
or kettle swung from a bracket. Upstairs was
an old bedstead, but the children not infre-
quently slept on chaff beds laid on the floor.
Many of the cottages had only two rooms, one

upstairs, the other down. So long as faggots and furze could be had for cutting some of the women made bread, not entirely from wheat-meal, but a mixture with barley-meal. This, with fat bacon, potatoes, onions, and small beer, was the staple food both of the labourers and small farmers. The labourer was not allowed to keep either a pig or fowls. The few shillings saved at hay-time and harvest-time was spent in paying off debts incurred during the winter or in buying clothes. A good smock frock, a heavy pair of watertight boots, corduroy breeches and waistcoat, a hard felt hat, leather gaiters which reached the thighs, made the usual outfit of a single man. But the man with a wife and family was often poorly clothed. A new smock frock and a pair of boots at Michaelmas was as much as he could afford.

I began to see that I had exchanged one kind of wretchedness for the prospect of another. A soldier who lodged in the village seemed to have a better time of it than a labourer, and as soon as my grandmother died, and I was old enough, I thought of enlisting into the Royal Rug-me-Dugs, the distinguished regiment to which I was told this young fellow belonged. Two or three young men had been persuaded against the tears and entreaties of their mothers to enlist, and they went swaggering about the village for a few days with ribbons and a drum. About a week after my arrival I was taken by my grandmother to an old woman to be measured for two smock frocks, one, a slaty colour, for week-days and an olive-green for Sundays, both artistically worked back and front. When she had finished measuring me she said, "Poor little fellow, I never thought he would come to this." The village shoemaker made the boots and gaiters, and in a fortnight after my arrival everything was provided. Up to this time I had lived with my grandmother, who, from declining health and age, could no longer be troubled with me. But there was great difficulty in finding a lodging, and the only place that offered was with an old couple in the almshouse, who had once occupied a farm in the parish, and were much respected. The man was unable to move, and sat all day in an armchair wearing a straw hat. His wife, a kind old woman, was troubled with rheumatism.

The winter evenings were very dull. No amusing book or interesting conversation to help the weary hours between dark and bed-time, which was soon after seven. The old woman with whom I lodged used occasionally to relate stories about witches, ghosts, will-o'-wisps, warlocks, and elfins that frightened me. She described their localities with accuracy, and her poor paralysed husband corroborated her stories in every particular. I had seen curious phenomena which I could not explain. I remember early one November morning I had gone into a low meadow to fetch the cows, and in the distance I saw two or three luminous bodies rising and falling, moving about, disappearing, and at short intervals reappearing. I only felt safe when the last cow passed through the gate into the road. Just as the morning began to break the luminous bodies disappeared. I told my story, and found that these things preferred living in wet meadows. Many years after I used to make these will-o'-wisps as a chemical experiment. They occur in nature from the decomposition of animal matter containing phosphorus.

At half-past five on Monday morning, when the larks were singing over the grave of my mother, which I passed on my way to work, and all nature seemed joyous and happy, I went to the Bury Farm, which was kept by a distant relation, and commenced my agricultural life by feeding some young pigs, collecting eggs, scrubbing the milk pails inside and out with a wisp of straw and wood ashes and fine sand until they were fit for a drawing-room, the iron bands shining like silver. Then came the wooden trenchers and bowls used for meals. On the dresser were rows of pewter plates and dishes, used in hay-time and harvest when the men had their food in the fields. There were twenty "leads" of milk in the dairy, and these had to be cleaned and scoured each time they were used. The skim milk went to the pigs. My previous domestic training made me useful about the house. In the afternoon I chopped up faggots for the fire and the oven, which was heated on Tuesdays and Thursdays. Twice a week I had to turn a small barrel-churn, but if elfins or witches were inside the butter was a long time in coming, and warm water had to be poured inside to drive them out. They are now expelled with a thermometer. It was springtime. The earth with its kingcups and cowslips, and the air filled with the song of birds, made it a second paradise—type of eternal life to me was the blessed spring! After a fortnight I was sent into the fields to pull docks, cut thistles, break clods, and scare birds. The latter was often solitary work. I have been for hours and sometimes days in the fields and not seen a human being. I used to eat my food by the sun, and if I had been instructed with the same care in some of the phenomena of nature as I was instructed in catechisms I should always have had a companion in my solitude. The foundation of all science and all knowledge is nature, but I remained in solitary ignorance.

After I had been at work at the Bury Farm three weeks I was moved on to the Hill

Farm. It was the custom for all who were not permanently attached to a farm to go the rounds, which meant that you worked on every farm in the parish either three weeks, nine days, or even two days, according to the acreage, and there were always a few going the rounds in the winter. The number was often eight or nine. If no work could be obtained after visiting all the farms, you worked on the roads, but you had to go the rounds every morning. At the Hill Farm I was sent to drive plough. I regarded this as a high promotion. To ride a mile on a horse in the grey twilight, with a long whip and a bag on one hime, with a bacon dumpling and a chunk of bread, and on the other a small wooden bottle of small beer, was the perfection of happiness. The ploughman was kind and good-natured, better than some of the plough-men at the Bury Farm, who were cruel to the horses, swore and used coarse language. I had no experience in driving plough, but the proper words for directing the horses were not difficult to learn, and for the first day or two were given by the ploughman. About eleven o'clock—guessed by the sun or the number of furrows ploughed—the horses had a feed, and the ploughman and I sat together on the plough beam. After he had drank his horn of beer from the wooden bottle he said, "John, my boy, I am sorry to see you here; and if your grandfather had been a wise man and your father a sober man, instead of ploughing other people's land, you might have been ploughing your own." My father at this time lived a few miles away, and so little did I know of him that had I met him in the street I should not have recognised him.

The neighbours always treated me with more kindness than other boys who had fathers and mothers, and, what was more important, I had enough to eat. The days I spent at plough were pleasant—the fragrance of the upturned earth was like the breath of spring. I was much struck with the quietness of the ploughman, for he seldom spoke, never whistled, or swore like some of the labourers. He used to give out verses of hymns, such as "Be it my only wisdom here," "A charge to keep I have," "And am I born

to die?" "The Lord Jehovah reigns," "Come
on, my partners in distress," and then to sing
them in a low tone of voice, and appeared
happy, although his singing was far from
being cheerful or musical.

I regretted when my round at the Hill
Farm came to an end, and I now moved on
to the Church Farm. The hay-time had just
begun. Scattering the fresh-cut grass, tend-
ing, cocking, and all the other operations of
haymaking are most enjoyable. Who would
exchange the life of an agricultural labourer, if
he were only decently housed and fed as he
ought to be, for that of a factory hand or a
miner or a docker? I now went for a few
days to the Grove Farm, and was employed
in hoeing and weeding. Now and then I
came across a partridge's nest. This was the
most sacred thing on the land. I was told if
I touched one I should be transported for life.
I now returned to the Bury Farm, and here I
remained the whole of the harvest. Instead
of going into the field with a sickle, as I
hoped, I was kept as house boy. I scrubbed
the potatoes, washed the vegetables, heated

the oven, and kept the copper fire going.
The dumplings, bacon, and cabbages were all
cooked together in a copper, which diffused
a fragrant atmosphere through the house.
Between eleven and twelve o'clock I harnessed
the donkey. The smoking bacon, vegetables,
bread, dumplings, pewter plates, and beer
were carefully wrapped up and packed in the
donkey-cart for the field. On my arrival the
men and boys ceased work and sat down in
some suitable place for dinner. It was my
business during the harvest to attend to the
eating and drinking; and if you want to enjoy
your food, get hungry by outdoor work, and
eat your dinner under the shade of a hawthorn hedge. The men in the rickyard dined
in the house.

The harvest began early but continued late;
it was not until October that the last load was
brought to the rickyard; and in some fields the
beans remained out till the middle of November. Most of the farmers had kept their
harvest-home, but ours was to come, and as
the farm was the largest the harvest-home
was the grandest. The farmer, his wife, and

their relations and friends sat at the top table, which was a little elevated; the men and boys sat at tables at right angles. At the sound of a horn the farmer said grace. The tables were loaded with smoking hot beef, mutton, bacon, geese, and plum-puddings. The ale was poured out of large leather jugs into horns, and was brewed for the occasion. In its way it was as grand a sight as anything at the Mansion House. Happily no one could make speeches or drink healths, but a few toasts such as " Success to the hoof and the horn," and " Success to the growers of corn." These and other toasts were received with boisterous rounds of applause, which increased with the quantity of ale consumed. Songs were sung of a national and patriotic and pastoral character, and when the refrain or chorus came, " To rip and sow and plough and mow and be a varmer's boy," the doors and windows vibrated. One man, a local preacher, didn't know a song and he was pressed for a hymn, which he sang, and was loudly applauded. The men who came from a distance slept in a barn which was comfortably littered down with clean straw, and some, for reasons other than distance, thought it better to remain the night. The next few days were occupied in boiling the pewter with nettles and setting things in order for the next year.

The autumn was now advancing, and the farm servants changed places. They stood about the streets of a neighbouring town, some with a piece of whipcord in their hats to show they were horsekeepers, others with wool to show they were shepherds, and others with cowhair to show they were cowmen. The farmers hired their men-servants for twelve-months; they lived in the house, and their wages were from five to ten pounds.

The village feast or carnival was held early in October, and all farm work in the parish ceased about twelve o'clock. Friends came to see friends, and there was much feasting. An open space in front of the village inn was the centre of attraction. Here the shows were drawn up—the golden farmer in wax, the learned pig that could play cards, a fat lady, a cheap Jack, and a sweetmeat and gingerbread stall, a mouth-organ and a drum. A gipsy with a fiddle sat on a platform and directed the dancing, which was active and vigorous; the men, with their smock frocks off, and the girls, with red and yellow ribbons, swinging backwards and forwards, panting, laughing, and perspiring, until the club-room became unsavoury. Towards dusk the men became noisy and valiant : one of them could lick six Frenchmen before breakfast, or any man from Norcot.

Now Norcot was a neighbouring village, and there had existed for years a feud between Norcot and Claywick, but how it originated or what it was all about no one knew. The Norcot men came to Claywick feast, and the Claywick men went to Norcot feast, to settle their yearly differences. Without two or three fights, the feast would have been an insipid failure. At Norcot there was a fighting family of the Pounders, and at Claywick there were the Clinchers, three brothers, who boasted they had never been beaten by a Norcot Pounder and never would. From one feast to another these men were the subject of village talk—they were respected and feared. Mr. Tapper, the perpetual curate, took a great interest in the Clinchers; it was said they were the only parishioners in whom he did take an interest. Suddenly there was a rush and a wild scream from the women, and in a few minutes half the population of Claywick was in a field at the back of the inn. Nothing could be seen except by those close to the performers, but the blows and applause could be heard for some distance.

The curate-in-charge was there, giving friendly suggestions and hints to the Clinchers through the parish clerk. After about half an hour one of the Clinchers was carried, all battered and bleeding, into the kitchen. Here the women applied fomentations and marsh-mallow leaves and herb ointments and poultices, but days passed before he could see. After the excitement of the feast had passed away, and to preserve the traditional pluck of Claywick, boys were often set to fight when at work in the fields, and encouraged by the men to get ready for the Pounders. I was once obliged to fight, but I never liked it. I could not see the fun of being hurt for the amusement of others, so I preferred being a coward with a whole skin.

The winter was coming on and I was anxious for a permanent place. I knew all the labourers and had worked with most of them on every farm in the parish. I was a favourite with the wife of the farmer at the Hill Farm, and she persuaded her husband to take me on at two shillings a week. In spring and summer and occasionally far into the autumn the country looks beautiful, but when the trees have shed their russet and golden leaves, and the cold north winds and rain and shortened days of winter set in, farm life has its trials. The stubble had to be ploughed up for the summer fallow; every three years the land was fallowed for the purpose of cleaning. Ploughing heavy clay land, and preparing it for the autumn-sown corn, was anything but agreeable. I have been at plough in winter with five and six horses one after the other, when lumps of clay used to stick to my feet, making it difficult to draw one leg after the other, so that our movements were very slow.   There were three, and occasionally four, persons with one plough —the ploughman, the driver, and another to clean the coulter and ploughshare at the head-lands ; these latter were generally boys. What a joy it was to get off this stiff clay and walk on to the green sward ! I was chiefly occupied during the winter in pulling turnips, carrying fodder, often before daybreak, folding the sheep, and cutting brushwood.   My hands were so swollen and chilled that I was glad of an opportunity of thrusting them between the collar and shoulder of a horse for a little warmth.   My shoes, heavily tipped, carried away the heat from my body, and I suffered during the winter from wet and cold. This is why farm labourers are often doubled up with rheumatism and unfit for work at a time when other persons comfortably off are in the prime of manhood.

When St. Thomas's Day was passed I anxiously watched the days lengthen.   Still January and February are often the coldest months, but the days increase in length. When the rooks began housekeeping pleasant hopes of barley-sowing and sheep-shearing and haymaking made me gradually forget the cold and storm of winter. How some of the boys who were poorly clad and fed pulled through the winter was a mystery. After two or three years I knew the ordinary routine of farm work as well as any farmer. Such agricultural knowledge as they had, and which many now have, is not deep, but no industry depends on such varied knowledge as the proper cultivation of the earth, and yet there is no industry in which you find so great a belief in custom and pure ignorance.

CHAPTER III.

MR. TAPPER, the curate-in-charge, used
occasionally to borrow me for a week.
He lived in the Rectory, the best house
in the parish, and was single, but kept a
housekeeper, a little girl, and a crookbacked
old man to attend to the glebe, look after
the fighting-cocks and a broken-winded old
horse, to which duties he joined the digging
of graves, tolling the bell, and occasionally
saying in church, "Lord, have mercy upon

us." He was always talking to himself and saying, " Amen, so be it." There was a general impression that this old man was harmlessly cracked. Both in church and out of church he was always jabbering, sometimes about his being robbed of his rights by the Archbishop and of his land by a neighbour. Then he would go off about the Pounders— when they won they never hit fair. He was a strange companion, but quite harmless. He worked hard, talking to himself all the time. One day I asked, " How was it you did not get your property ? " He replied, " Your father knows why I didn't get it, he was at the trial. The judge said my brother was the rightful owner, and he kept me out of it."

The living was worth about five hundred pounds a year, a good house and garden, and twelve acres of glebe. It was in the gift of one of the Oxford Colleges, and was held by one of the Fellows, whom few had seen. About August Mr. Tapper used to spend two or three days with the rector at a country inn, about halfway between Claywick and Oxford. The church was an old Norman structure, cold and damp, and the walls covered with lichen. The building was fast falling into ruin; no one cared about it, and service inside was rather intermittent. The boys stole the lead from the windows and gutters to make chequers.

With all my faults I was regarded, next to Mr. Tapper, the best educated in the parish, because I could read and had some knowledge of writing. Mr. Tapper would occasionally borrow me only for a day or two, but our intercourse was always pleasant. I had a sort of reverence for him because he was the rector and could read Latin and Greek books, and some said he had the Hebrew Bible of Moses. Mr. Tapper and I used to work together in the field and garden, and his conversation was full of good advice. He used to say, "John, be what you like. I don't say come to church, because I don't want to offend your old grandmother, but don't be a Methodist, they tell lies and are no good. Why don't they convert Tom Parrott, a notorious drunkard and poacher in the village?" He thought the Quakers worse than the Methodists; they objected to tithes, church rates, Easter dues, and paid parsons.

This brought to my memory a scene I had witnessed as a child. The curate-in-charge before Mr. Tapper and the head-borough were superintending the loading of a cart with a miscellaneous collection of things taken from two houses. There was some excitement, angry words, and threats. The curate said something about obeying the law, and as the cart moved off there was a good deal of hooting and yelling, especially from the women. The goods were removed to a neighbouring town for sale. It would have been impossible to sell them in the parish, and it was not easy to sell them anywhere where people knew to whom they belonged. I had a vague idea that these things were taken because people would not go to church. I knew nothing about Church rates.

I was told some years after that an ancestor of mine was sent to prison because he refused to pay tithe. The churchwarden, who had some difference with the curate about gravelling a path which led to the church, brought, out of pure ill-nature, some Methodist preachers into the village. No one but the parish clerk stood by the curate, and all sorts of disagreeable things were circulated about him: he didn't preach the gospel; the church was no good to any one, it only robbed them of the charities; the curate was a whited sepulchre; he had never experienced the influence of converting grace; he was the blind leading the blind. The result was that no one went to church, and for weeks the door was never unlocked.

But this state of things never disturbed Mr. Tapper; his short, plump figure could be seen walking leisurely through the village on Sunday in a low-crowned beaver hat, knee-breeches with gaiters to match, a buff waistcoat, a yellow silk neckcloth, and a blue coat with buttons which some said were made of gold taken from the parish charities and the sales of goods taken for tithes and church rates.

In the summer-time the Methodists walked backwards and forwards through the village on Sundays singing hymns, and as no room could be obtained, except the kitchen of the late churchwarden, the preaching and praying were conducted in the open air. During the winter the labourers had prayer-meetings and class-meetings in their cottages. Any one could attend, but the rooms were small and stuffy. I occasionally went to their meetings to pass away the evening, but the ranting and groaning and the confessions of some of the converted were frightful. I had no idea I had been living and working with men who ought to have been in prison. Their interjectory remarks appeared to me sinful. They talked familiarly about Jesus Christ, as if He were a farm labourer keeping a family on nine shillings a week. He was invited to come among them in a chariot of fire and water His people with a holy waterpot. " Brush us with Thy heavenly besom and we shall be clean." If all the "Amens" and the "Lords have mercy upon us" were taken out of their service there was not much left. All this puzzled me, yet I felt there was something in it. The hymns I thought the best part of the service, and as they were read out two lines at a time, many of the more popular of them were soon committed to memory. Since the Restoration these men had been left without any religion, and as men cannot live without some sort of religion, the Methodists provided one. It had its good side as well as its grotesque side : it gave these poor men something to think about; it gave them comfort in time of want and suffering; it was to them the only thing which made this life tolerable, with the hope of a better; and their example often checked licentiousness in others. As far as it went, it was a civilising and humanising influence. The trials and temptations to which such men were exposed found relief in the weekly prayer-meeting or class-meeting and hymns, and their earnest appeals to the Lord for strength showed their sincerity.

But there was a bad time in store for the Methodists : it had been rumoured that these prayer - meetings were more political than religious. The landlords and some of the farmers were prayed for by name. "Cursed is he who removeth his neighbour's landmark, and oppresseth the poor and needy, and joineth land to land," and stoppeth footpaths; these sentences always met with hearty amens.

If there be one man of a party a little better educated than the others and mentally their superior, and there is nothing against his moral life, and if in addition he has a deep religious conviction, that man becomes the leader of his party. He is not elected to it, no one appoints him, but he is looked up to by others, and exercises power of which he is not conscious. Such a man was the Claywick shoemaker. He had gone deeper into Arminianism and politics than any of his fellows. The *Methodist Magazine* and the *Weekly Dispatch* were regularly sent to him by his brother. He always had plenty of shoemaking, and was more independent than either the farmers or labourers. He used to make uncivil remarks about the landlords and the House of Lords, the House of Commons, the new poor law, bishops, parsons, Corn Laws, the church, and class legislation. It was reported that he constantly referred to these things in his prayers. But everybody knew him to be a just, upright man who made the best boots in the county. He had to pay a small annual tithe and rent, which were received at the village inn by the lawyers to the Trinkwasser estate. Mr. Tapper was in the chair. The table was well furnished with cold beef, chine, ham, cheese, bread, ale, tobacco, and pipes for those who came to pay; and some said that those who had only one-and-sixpence or two shillings to pay never would have paid if they could not have taken it out in eating and drinking.

I saw the shoemaker hurrying down the street, and he asked me to accompany him. I had no tithes or rent to pay, and had no business at the meeting. As soon as we entered the room everybody stared at the shoemaker, and Mr. Tapper whispered to the Trinkwasser lawyers as he walked up to the table dressed in an olive-green smock-frock and gaiters; a tall, well-made man, with eyes, when excited, that went through you. He took from his pocket a yellow linen purse, twisted at the top like a sack of wheat, and counted out one-and-sixpence in pence and placed it on the table, and said : " Give me a receipt. I pay this under protest ; it is a robbery. Tithes were abolished by order of Melchisedec."

There were faint manifestations of applause.
Mr. Tapper said this disaffection in the parish
was due to the spread of Methodism, and he
hoped it would not be repeated. When the
tithes and rent had been paid the men
settled down to their pipes, and Mr. Tapper
made a speech about the growing disregard of
the Church and resistance to constitutional
authority among the labouring classes, refusing to render unto Cæsar the things which
belonged to Cæsar. The shoemaker had great
difficulty in keeping quiet. He wanted to reply
to Mr. Tapper's speech, but his friends dis-
suaded him. After Mr. Tapper came the
agent for the Trinkwasser property. He
lamented with Mr. Tapper the gradual aliena-
tion of the agricultural labourers from their
best friends, the landlords and the clergy.
The pernicious doctrines of the manufacturing districts had been sown broadcast by
tracts and paid agitators, setting class against
class; and recently an agitation had sprung
up in Manchester which attacked the agricultural interest with the most unscrupulous
falsehoods, and if not checked, as it would be,

by force if necessary, could only end in the complete ruin of the agriculturalist. It was proposed to abolish the duty on the importation of wheat, which meant ruin to the landlords, ruin to the farmers, and starvation for the labourers. The land must go out of cultivation. It had been reported, on good authority, that in the event of any reduction of the duty on the importation of foreign-grown wheat from countries where there were no rates or taxes or burdens on land, and where the labourers lived on black bread and worked for twopence a day, the landowners would sell their estates, break up their establishments, and go to America or some other country. In reply to this the shoemaker stood up and shouted out: "A devilish good thing—I should like to see it!"

The constable was ordered to remove him, and the shoemaker walked out and I followed. In a few minutes he settled down to his work and began violently hammering a piece of leather on the lapstone. When he was annoyed the sole leather was well hammered, while he recited the petty persecutions going on in the village and neighbourhood—the enclosure of Claywick common and strips of land on the roadside, the extermination of small farmers. No one knew how it was, but everything that went on in the village was known to the trustees, except the winter wretchedness and poverty, which they disregarded.

The prayer-meetings and class-meetings at the shoemaker's had to be abandoned on pain of ejectment; the shoemaker had notice to quit. He left the cottage of his forefathers, and in a few weeks it was pulled down, and his piece of land added to a farm. Some began to say that all this trouble had been brought about by his remarks at the rent audit. He ought to have kept his tongue quiet before the trustees; and one or two of his staunchest supporters turned against him, and others spoke disparagingly of him. What they most wanted was their prayer-meetings, and the Methodists were divided on the conduct of the shoemaker. The younger Methodists supported him, the elder Methodists were against him. For some time nothing was talked about but the eviction and the probable eviction of others. The suppression of the prayer-meetings commended itself to Mr. Tapper and the sexton, but when a few men think they have the germ of any kind of religion it fertilises and strengthens under injustice and persecution.

The men used to meet and hold their prayer-meetings in barns, rickyards, and outbuildings, and new converts were added, until Methodism became a factor in the parish. In the summer they could sing, pray, and exhort out of doors; but in winter the want of a room was sadly felt. Three or four would meet in one cottage and some in another. They were advised to make their prayers sitting with their eyes shut, so that they could say there was no prayer-meeting because no one knelt. They would sometimes sit for an hour without uttering anything but groans. They began to feel that they could hold communion with God quite as much as in their more noisy and boisterous demonstrations. Great was the rejoicing when Master Johnson became converted. He had a freehold cottage and a large garden, and he cheerfully gave up a portion of the latter for a Methodist chapel;

and in six months it was opened with all the bass-viols, fiddles, flutes, and clarionets of the neighbourhood. It was, of course, ugly; but that was of no consequence. At one end there was a gallery for the musicians, and the music, such as it was, filled the chapel and made the service attractive. I used to help the shoe-maker part of the way home with his bass-viol. He talked about the sermon, which was not so good as it might have been. No reference was made to their persecutions, and the doctrine of free-will was not mentioned.

Every now and again there was the threatening or persecution of somebody, and this kept up a spirit of resistance and un-rest. Incendiary fires became frequent in the neighbourhood, and this only increased the general discontent, some saying openly that a few more fires would do good. For-tunately, a circumstance occurred which more than anything else changed the whole state of affairs. One of the farmers who had emigrated some years ago to America wrote a glowing account of the country and its prospects, urging all who could to come over to Iowa. The letter was read in almost every cottage. It was read at the village inn and at the Methodist chapel every Sunday until it was nearly worn out. The Lord had now opened a door of escape. Special prayer-meetings were held to know the Lord's will, which was that they should go. For several weeks nothing was thought about or talked about but going to America. The whole village was at work in packing and mending clothes. A farewell service was held in the Methodist chapel, which was crowded, and the services lasted through night till day-break. The following evening, in the glorious springtime of May, some thirty-three men, women, and children knelt down in the street, and, after a short prayer-meeting, marched through the village singing hymns. The whole village turned out, and many accompanied them for miles. " Good-bye ; God bless you !" rang from every cottage door. Every eye was wet. Mr. Tapper leaned over the Rectory gate and was visibly affected with this melancholy procession of his best parishioners. Prayers in the Methodist chapel were

regularly offered up for the exiles until news
came of their safe arrival and settlement.
This induced others, in batches of threes and
fours, to follow for several years.

Old Diggins, the sexton, had fallen ill, and
I went to the Rectory to supply his place.
Almost everybody in the parish had fallen out
with Mr. Tapper, but I was a boy and never
pretended to serious differences with grown-
up men, nor had I ever joined other boys in
making noises, or whistled when Mr. Tapper
spoke at any meeting. He was always friendly
and communicative with me. We used to
work on the glebe and in the garden together.
It was evident he abhorred the shoemaker and
Radicals and Dissenters, especially Methodists
and Quakers, who were, he said, a lying, hypocritical lot. Mr. Tapper regretted there was
no school for boys like me and a few others in
the parish, and he was willing, if we wished, to
teach us. It was summer-time, and I spoke to
some of my companions, who were the sons of
small farmers, and they were willing, when the
harvest was over, to go to the Rectory and be
taught to read and write. Mr. Tapper used

to smoke his pipe, make us do sums, and write and spell words of two syllables. I was more advanced than the others because I had been to school, and Mr. Tapper used to teach me alone, and we were all thankful for what he taught. After two winters we were up to the third standard, and that was something for boys who knew nothing.

Mr. Tapper occasionally went to a church two or three miles off, and I used to go with him and hold his horse while he read prayers. The horse was an old broken-winded " toast-rack." I sat behind with my fingers stuck into a leather belt which Mr. Tapper wore round his waist when on horseback. We could have walked the distance in less time if Mr. Tapper had been less bulky. The church was on one side of the road and the Cock Inn on the other. It was kept by the churchwarden, who was also a small farmer. Mr. Tapper first went into the " Cock " to hear the news and scandal about Mrs. So-and-so's daughter coming home to be confined, which was not an uncommon occur-rence. It not unfrequently happened that there was no congregation. Either the weather was too cold or too hot or too wet. If half a dozen persons were present I had to inform Mr. Tapper; but this number was not always reached. On one occasion it was exceeded, and I exercised the horse round the churchyard. His hunting capabilities were gone, and he preferred the slow movements of old age. Once he attempted to jump a low gravestone and failed. As I passed round the churchyard on horseback I could see into the church. Mr. Tapper, who spoke to me through the window, said, " John, you had better tighten the girth ; " he then went on with the service. These journeys for eight months in the year were most enjoyable, and always ended with a good supper at the Rectory, when Mr. Tapper used to make Latin quotations and smoke his pipe. The Latin was lost on me, but I believe it always had reference to somebody or something in the village.

CHAPTER IV.

ONE Sunday evening I met the shoemaker returning from the Methodist chapel, and I walked part of the way home with him. He was boiling over with wrath at his being turned out of a home in which his grandfather, who carried on the same business, was born and died. He told me a large meeting was shortly to be held on the Downs

about ten miles distant, and men were coming
from Birmingham and other towns to put an
end to tyranny and rotten boroughs and
landlords. He asked if I should like to go,
and I readily assented. I thought I knew
what tyranny was, but I did not know what
a rotten borough was like. Early one May
morning I started with two or three others in
an old farm-cart for the Downs. On the road
there passed other carts and waggons crowded
with passengers; some had flags and music.
As we drew near to the Downs the procession
and excitement increased. On a slight elevation you could see a number of waggons.
This was the centre of the gathering. The
fringe of the Downs was occupied with conjurors, political ballad-singers and players,
and gingerbread-stalls. Two men, dressed
like Mr. Tapper when he read the burial
service, with square black caps, like what I
had seen hanging up at the Rectory, were
reciting a kind of litany. One would say,
" Let us pray." " O Lord, save us from all
priests and kings; they live and fatten on
the labour of slaves." " O Wellington, have

mercy upon us." "Sidmouth, hear us." "From rotten boroughs and boroughmongers, good Lord, deliver us"; and so on. The men said, "We are not allowed to sell these prayers, but we sell a straw for a penny and give you the prayers." I should have purchased a straw, but I had no money.

With two or three others whom I knew we pressed forward to the waggons from a little elevation on the Downs. The sight was impressive. As far as the eye could carry, along every road and footpath, there was a living stream flowing towards the committee waggon. The flags and banners had on sentences, such as, "No pensions for royal concubines!" "Down with the House of Lords!" "Taxation without representation is a tyranny which ought to be resisted!" "Workhouses for the poor and palaces and pensions for the rich!" "More pigs and fewer parsons!" "He saw the people were oppressed and He smote their oppressors!" All this was very confusing, and I had no idea what it meant. About midday thousands of people were assembled, and they still kept flowing in. I had no idea there were so many people in the world. But when I saw soldiers coming out of the woods on the fringe of the Downs, some on horseback, others walking backwards and forwards, armed with guns and swords, I began to be frightened. The people called out, " Are we in for another Peterloo?" Officers in cocked hats galloped round and round.

The men were speaking from different waggons. I stood on the wheel of one from which a man in his shirt-sleeves, with black eyes and hair, said he was a stockinger, and earned nine shillings a week when he had work. He had a wife and three children to keep. He went in strong, vigorous language at everything—kings, bishops, parsons, and landlords. He had been in prison and was ready to go again if the tyrants wished it. He said the Church and State had entered into a partnership. One said, " You enslave their bodies, and we will enslave their minds." The red-coats were vampires, thirsting for the blood of poor, defenceless people. He occasionally swore—so help me God! I had never heard or read such language, and as he went

on his wild eyes and expression terrified me.
The people who came with me were lost in
the crowd, and I could find neither the cart
nor the horse that brought us. I was afraid
there would be a battle. The people were
getting more noisy and the soldiers more
active, and as I had no wish to be killed
for what I did not understand, I started for
home.

One man told me there would be no fighting that day; when it did begin it would be
all over the country. I had no idea as to the
road for Claywick, and after walking two or
three miles, which might have been in the
wrong direction, I made my way to a farmhouse for inquiry. A man came out using
the most horrid oaths, language, and threatening to blow my brains out if I did not move
off, which I did as quickly as possible. Some
distance off, on the low hillside, I saw a
shepherd making his fold, and I made for
him. I found I had not come far out of my
way. He asked about the meeting. "We,"
said he, "saw the horse marines [yeomanry]
pass early in the morning." He asked if I

belonged to the E. H. A. I replied, " No."
" 'Spose you are too young." Some time
after I found that these letters were the password of a secret society, which was changed
every few months. The shepherd took me to
his cottage and gave me some bread and cold
chitterlings, which was the only food I had
tasted since seven o'clock. He put me on the
road.

I arrived at Claywick soon after dark. I
went to bed, weary and tired, and began to
wonder what had become of the shoemaker
and others, but I soon fell asleep. Early the
following morning I was awakened by the
shoemaker, who had been seeking for me the
whole night. The next day I was due at
Mr. Tapper's, and I was told by the shoemaker not to say a word to any one that I
had been with him to the meeting, or what I
had seen and heard. A few days after a
parson called on Mr. Tapper when we were
working together in the garden, and I heard
them talking about the meeting and the disturbed state of the country. On the night of
the meeting the rickyard and outbuildings of

the Manor Farm were burned down, and from the description I thought it must be the farm at which I had called a few days before.

Weeks passed by, and I was now at clover cart with the man for whom I had driven plough at the Hill Farm. We saw a man looking over the gate, and then get over and walk towards us. This was such an unusual thing that we left off work and glared at him. On his coming up he asked me if I was the boy who called at the Manor Farm on the day of the great meeting. I said I did not know the name of the farm, but the man threatened to shoot me. He said, "You must come with me to Mr. Blase," who was a parson and a magistrate who lived four miles off, and had the reputation of being one of the cruellest men, especially to poachers. I began to cry. My companion came from the other side of the cart, and said, "If you lay hands on the boy, I'll run this pitchfork through you!" He walked off, and I was thankful. I never saw him again.

Things now quieted down for a time, and the village resumed its usual sleepy condition.

Suddenly one evening the village was thrown into a state of panic. Twenty or thirty drunken soldiers, some with side-arms, broke into the village inn, smashed the windows, helped themselves to drink, threw the pots out of the window, and violently beat a kettle-drum. Everybody was in a state of fear and panic. Some said they had just come from France, where they had been killing French-men, and they meant to go on killing some-body. They wore black shakos, with a round red ball of worsted on the top, and their uni-form was nearly black. Their clothes and hats and belts were scattered about the street. Presently the constable, in a smock-frock and gaiters, arrived. Mr. Tapper was already on the scene with a pair of horse pistols, but it was thought better not to interfere. After some time most of them moved off, but a few who were too drunk to walk or lie down were locked up for the night in a stable, to be taken before Mr. Blase the following morning. The women and some of the men were in fear that they might break out in the night and murder the whole village. The door and window were strengthened with extra pieces of timber, and everything was made secure.

The following morning was looked for with great interest. The civil and spiritual authority was increased by constables and parsons from neighbouring villages. The constable looked through the key-hole, and quietly introduced the key. The plan of attack was for the constables to suddenly rush in with staves and handcuffs, while Mr. Tapper was to remain outside the door with pistols, and Joe Mullens was to stand opposite with an old sword. The flank and rear were supported by a few labourers, who asked Mr. Tapper for some beer to drink the King's health. When the attacking party rushed in they found all the prisoners had escaped through an iron grating into a field, and were nowhere to be seen. Claywick again relapsed into its sleepy condition.

One Sunday afternoon Mr. Tapper took me and the other boys who formed his evening school to see the making of the London and North-Western Railway, when I saw that all hills were made of chalk. We returned to the

Rectory to supper, and he gave us each a glass of port wine—the first I had ever tasted, and I thought it very good. We began to think that Mr. Tapper was not a bad sort, and if he had not been a parson—which perhaps he could not help—he would have been one of the most popular men in the parish. He used to say openly that the Methodists had no authority to preach; he spoke of their little chapel as a "schism shop" and a "conventicle"; their preachers were uneducated, low-bred, ignorant fellows, some of them unable to read; and the Quakers were not much better. Now these often-expressed opinions, in a parish where three-fourths of the people were Methodists if they were anything, and the other fourth nothing, were not likely to promote brotherly love between Mr. Tapper and his parishioners. I shall always feel grateful for his evening school and his Sunday morning school in summer, in the tower of the old church, where I first learned that the earth was like an orange and moved round the sun, and *luna* was Latin for moon. I fear the rising intellect of Claywick was not very bright, and the older intellect was of the earth earthy.

Three winters' frosts and snows and storms and three summers of hard work, sound sleep, and the purest of pleasures which move men to the love and admiration of nature, had now passed away. I was as familiar with the routine of agricultural work as if I had been there for a century. The labourers know as much about farming as the farmers, but the labourers never had the chance of showing it —they remained labourers. I knew the names of most of the field birds, where they built, and the colour of their eggs. I could find most nests, but a peewit's nest I never, found. Almost every barn had owls; and hawks were often busy among the small birds. The finest sport, quite equal to fox-hunting and not nearly so dangerous, was rat-hunting. Many of the corn-ricks, especially when built upon the ground, were often riddled from top to bottom with rats. When these ricks were taken into the barn for thrashing there was fine sport. With sticks and dogs we used to chase them round the rickyard and knock them over by dozens.

One day, after one of these rat-hunts, as I was going home, I saw enormous blue bills stuck on every barn door and wall, and in some of the windows. As I passed the Rectory I saw Mr. Tapper was busy superintending the bill-sticking on the Rectory wall. These bills invited the free and independent electors to vote for Lords Candlemas and Rushlight, the tried farmers' friends, the firm friends of Church and State, the pledged supporters of protection to agriculture. I thought I should like to ask Mr. Tapper what all this meant, because I had never heard, except at the meeting on the Downs, that anybody in the village objected to these things except the shoemaker, and he had left. But the following day I saw him in the village. He was often backwards and forwards, bringing boots and measuring for new ones. His removal had rather increased his business, which some thought would be ruined. I asked him what protection to agriculture meant, and he replied, "My paying, and every other body paying, threepence or fourpence more for a loaf of bread for the benefit of a landed aristocracy."

Towards the fall of the year a few of us were invited to Norcot to supper with Master Bitson, who was a small proprietor and farmer. He had a considerable reputation as a Baptist preacher, and held forth every Sunday to a numerous congregation in an old barn, which was fitted up, and known for miles round as Bitson's Chapel. He always had a self-satisfied smile. You could read in his face, "I am all right." His preaching was always personal and rude, which the people liked. Here is a sample: "Jim Meade, I hear, is about to take to himself a wife; but unless he has plenty of fat with her, in a few years they will be in the workhouse, with a swarm of children for me and others to keep, poor fools! Is this doing the Lord's will?" His criticisms on the Methodist religion were very severe. They were all wrong. Arminianism would not square with the inspired Word, and was no better, rather worse, than infidelity. A man cannot save himself. The Lord settles who shall be saved. After a long sermon, all, of course, extempore—for he could not have written a sermon — we listened to a long grace while the beef and dumplings were getting cold. When Bitson was wound up, either for a prayer or a sermon, no one knew when he was likely to finish. During the grace before beef one of the boys, whose father had just taken a farm in the adjoining parish, and was a stranger, was seen to cross himself. I had never seen persons cross themselves except when they expected ghosts. Bitson opened his eyes, - and went at this poor lad like a tiger— preached a sermon on the sin of idolatry, and how Jeroboam, the son of Nebat, had sinned. All the time the beef was getting cold. But old Bitson was hot! "Go out of this habitation, thou son of Belial!" he cried. The poor boy burst into tears, and went sorrowfully home without his supper. I felt for this lad as, thank God, I have always felt for uncalled-for attacks on defenceless innocence.

I was now over thirteen years of age, and the prospect of a journeyman farmer was not very inviting, and from a few casual remarks I had an idea that I should shortly have to make a change. I knew that my uncle had an interview with my father, and I heard shortly after that I was to be apprenticed, but not to my uncle. The idea of being bound for seven years to the man I loathed, who, a few years before, had me measured for a coffin, was too horrible; but my apprenticeship to any person but a relative was more hopeful. My mother was dead, my grandmother was dead, my father I seldom saw, and when I did he scarcely spoke to me. So I turned my back on my native village, which I never visited again for nearly fifty years.

When I did visit it no one then knew me; everything had changed but the chalk hills. The labourers were a little better off, but the land was not much better tilled or more productive, except where it was drained. The flail was gone, the sickle was gone, and the scythe was going. The chief improvement was in implements, often the invention of men outside the farm. The labourers walked with the same slow, heavy gait, the result of clods they had to carry on their feet. Many of the birds had departed. There were no owls, magpies, jays, hawks, or kingfishers. All the small farms had quite disappeared. The homely but not always comfortable farm-houses had given way on the hillside to Gothic villas and mansions for stockbrokers, bankers, hunting men, and company pro-moters. The stock had improved, but the general unrest and desire for something better among the labourers remained. The Church had been restored, and a new Methodist chapel had been built in another part of the parish. The Church had made some head-way, chiefly through the school, which was taught by a devout and intelligent Church-woman. But her life was often lonely; she never went to the Rectory except on business. The farmers' wives and daughters thought her not good enough to associate with them, although she was better educated and more accomplished.

After walking round the field and hedgerows which I knew as a boy, I was making my way to the station when a woman came up and said, "I think Master Rickson would know you if you be Tom Buckley's boy." I asked where he lived. I made my way to the cottage where he lodged, and found him upstairs ill. He had been past work for two years, crippled with rheumatism and existing on 2s. 6d. a week. He was left to the care and kindness of neighbours as poor as himself. Poor Master Rickson! One of the early band of Methodists, he had borne the heat and burden of the day, and was now left in his last moments to the tender mercies of the parish and the kindness of his neighbours. I went up an old step-ladder through a trap-door into the roof; the thatch came within a few inches of the floor, and the light streamed through a small broken window at the end. On a bed, as far as I could see, made up of old boxes, on which was an old straw mattress, lay Master Rickson. By his side there was an old table with medicine bottles and a piece of untouched bread-and-butter and a teacup. He was covered with old pieces of horse rugs and sacking which had the name of Garner. I spoke to him, but he failed to recognise me; he feebly opened his glassy eyes and groaned, "Why has Thou forsaken me?" I saw the end was near. I had worked with this man when the lark ascended heavenwards. This was the man for whom I had driven plough; he had threatened to pitchfork a man in defence of me; he had consistently borne a religious life; and this was the end of it. I spoke to the old woman downstairs, who was making lace, as to his burial. She replied, " The parish always sees to that." I said, " Take that to Master Cutler, and when the time comes he will provide a decent funeral without the parish."

There was one other man for whom I had great respect, John Jebbs. In early life he had been what is known as a rackety young man. He became a Methodist, and entered on a new life. Methodism, like other systems, had no scientific basis; it was a Salvation Army movement, and was well suited to the condition of the illiterate. It urged men of their own free will to strive for a higher and better life, and any system which does this is a good thing, because in the striving men in some degree attain what they want. But for the hope of another life, which was one of punishment or reward, the condition of the agricultural labourer would have been worse than the beast of the field, for whom Providence provides food and clothing without much effort on their part. After a time John Jebbs became more reserved and melancholy, he seldom associated with others or went to class-meetings or prayer-meetings, he preferred being alone, and as he was much esteemed this wish was respected by his employers. He could be seen for days working alone in an open field, his flail could be heard early in the morning in some solitary barn. At hay-time and harvest-time, when the men were obliged to work together and have their food in the field, John Jebbs, as soon as his wooden trencher and horn of ale were filled, would retire a distance from the other men and eat his food alone. His gloomy silence inspired a respectful awe, because all believed him to be a good man. It was a great grief and the occasion of much prayer when he finally separated from the Methodists and went every Sunday—all weathers, a distance of four miles—to hear Master Bitson talk on pure, unadulterated Calvinism. I have heard him when he was sitting on the plough beam repeat to himself in a melancholy tone, "For the children being not yet born, neither having done any good or evil, that the purpose of God, according to election, might stand." John Jebbs had scarcely attained middle age when he was suddenly stricken down with a serious illness, and was taken home from the harvest field. His suffering for a time was very acute, but with fomentations of marsh mallow and drinking herb tea it was thought he would recover, but it was not to be. During his illness his former brother and sister Methodists seldom inquired after him or visited him; he had deserted them for another religion which in the eyes of some was worse than no religion. One evening in August one of the elders came over to see him; he was bolstered up in a chair under the walnut-tree. The elder said, "I am sent hither by God," and after a few remarks asked, "How do you feel about the blessed promises?" He replied, "I hope it is all right." "'Hope'!" replied the elder, raising his voice ; "that won't do. You must say, I know." It was a lovely autumn evening, the sun was sinking below the Chilterns, and John Jebbs sank with it, and passed quietly from what he did know to solve the problem of the unknown.

CHAPTER V.

IT was a lovely spring evening when a waggon, laden with pork, butter, eggs, boxes, and parcels, called at the " Waggoner's Arms " for John Buckley and a carpet bag. We had to travel through miles of lanes before we got into the high-road. We crossed the chalk hills, and in the prismatic glow of twilight the sun fell below the horizon and all nature was peaceful. It was one of those scenes which make men sorrow for the past and hope for the future. I had a heavy heart and grave doubts after the lanterns were lighted and hung about the waggon. I turned in and slept till sunrise, which by many is never seen, but is often more glorious than a sunset. A country waggon with its Norman roof of tarpaulin, except that it had no springs, was by no means a bad lodging. The morning was even more lovely than the evening; the birds were singing on the hedges and the larks flew upwards until they appeared like blowflies. I now took the whip and the waggoner took my bed. The journey was slow and tedious, because we had to deliver and take in at the different villages through which we passed. Towards evening I saw the smoke of Oxenbridge, and my heart sank. The waggoner saw I was depressed. I wanted to go back to Claywick; the memory of the past brought tears. He said, "Cheer up, my cockolorum, a joiner is better than a farm labourer."

I derived some comfort from the reflection that I was not to be apprenticed to my uncle, and it would not last for ever. On my arrival

the creature who had measured me for a coffin
met me with smiles and conducted me, not to
the house of the man to whom I was to be
apprenticed, but to the house of my former
sufferings and misery. I wished I had ran
away while the waggoner was asleep. I was
received with all the outward fulsome expressions of kindness. The girls sneered at my
language and smock-frock, which was more
artistic than their dresses. The evening was
occupied with advice and glowing prospects
of the future, and the brilliant career of
a good workman and ultimately a master.
I retired to the old cupboard of a bedroom,
which had been enlarged to make room for a
bench. The strong smell of shavings kept
me awake for a time, but weary, tired, and
heart-sore, I fell asleep. The next morning I
put on a flannel jacket and white apron and
went into the shop. One of the men taught
me to make a paper cap and my toilet was
complete. At eleven o'clock I was asked to pay
my footing. I had a few shillings which had
been collected for me before I left Claywick,
and most of this went in buying beer for the

men. I was told that I should have to do the same thing to-morrow because other men who were out at work would be in the shop, but the majority resented this as an imposition—one footing was the rule.

My first job was to turn the grindstone for the man who measured me for a coffin. How I loathed this wretch! He was now growing old, and I hoped he would soon die. I learned one thing, that grindstones for carpenter's and joiner's tools should always be worn from the outside, so as to keep the centre like the ridge of a house. If tools such as plane irons and chisels are ground in the middle of the stone it becomes hollow, and you cannot grind tools with straight edges on a hollow stone. Making the glue hot, cooking herrings and bacon, fetching beer and water, sweeping up the shavings, chopping wood, and waiting on the men, occupied nearly the whole of my time. Any interval was spent in planing floor boards and sawing slating battens. Every morning I had to be first to unlock the shop, and in the evening I had to lock-up. After all the men had left there were many little things to do, which generally occupied another hour. The regular time was ten hours a day, but this was often extended in a busy time to twelve and a half hours.

I had to count all the nails and screws, and measure and keep account of everything sent out of the yard. This kept me pretty well employed in a shop of twenty to thirty men, besides bricklayers, labourers, plasterers, painters, sawyers, and lathrenders. My time was at the service of all these men. In addition, I had to keep the men's time. My writing was bad, and my spelling of such words as "scaffold," "architrave," "brest-summer" was worse and often got me into trouble. I soon learnt the names and uses of all the tools. As a man without a good chest of tools was regarded as an inferior workman, perhaps fond of drink, the first desire of an apprentice is for a good chest of tools, and to take a pride in keeping them in first-rate condition. I soon grew familiar with the names of different sorts of nails, screws, hinges, locks, and bolts. A short time in contact with these things is a far easier way of learning them than any verbal description or even drawings.

After about two months there was some talk about my being bound apprentice. I should have been bound before, but my father had some difficulty in raising the fifty pounds. I was in no hurry to be apprenticed to one man and live with another. I had two masters, but so far I had no complaint, and as much liberty as my work would permit. I was not, as formerly, grudged my food, and no nasty remarks were made about my having a wolf in my stomach. I was paid a wage commencing at seven-and-sixpence a week, and rising in the last year to twenty-one shillings, the maximum wage of an average journeyman carpenter and joiner. My grandmother left me ten pounds for the purchase of tools. About two pounds were spent in buying second-hand tools, and I was robbed of the balance. One evening I had to appear at a lawyer's office with my master and uncle and father. The lawyer read over a long rigmarole called an indenture, which was the largest printed word on the parchment. I had gloomy forebodings as to the future, but

I had no heart to resist, and the next day I entered on a seven years' apprenticeship.

" This Indenture witnesseth John Buckley, of Claywick, son of Thomas Buckley, of Claywick, who of his own free will and accord, and by and with the consent and approbation of his father, doth put himself apprentice to Joseph Shapward, of Oxenbridge, to learn the art, trade, or business of a carpenter and joiner from the 1st of December, 1833, to the 1st of December, 1840. During his apprenticeship the said John Buckley shall go regularly to church, shall faithfully serve his master and keep all secrets, gladly do his lawful commands, shall not commit fornication nor contract matrimony within the said term of seven years, and shall not play at cards, dice, tables, or any other game of chance ; he shall neither buy nor sell, he shall not haunt taverns nor playhouses, keep bad company, nor absent himself from his said master's service day or night, and the said Joseph Shapward, in consideration of the sum of fifty pounds, doth covenant to teach his apprentice the art, trade, or business of a carpenter and joiner, finding the said apprentice sufficient meat, drink, and lodging, and for the due performance of every and all the said covenants and agreements, the said parties hereby bind themselves," &c., &c.

The next day after my apprenticeship I had to stand another footing, and now that I was an apprentice there were a few perquisites. All shavings not wanted by the men or in the house were mine, and were sold for twopence a sack. Rich persons who kept two servants paid threepence, and the Friends always paid threepence, but I had often to carry the shavings nearly a mile after work. My income from shavings averaged about fivepence a week, and this kept me in pocket-money, and it was all I had. The first Saturday I went into the counting-house for my money. At that time I did not know or had forgotten how much I was to receive. I was told that my wages would always be paid, according to agreement, to my uncle for board and lodging. This went through me like a dagger, but I was helpless.

One man in the shop, Master Bedford—

peace to his ashes!—always spoke kindly to me. He knew how I was situated, and his words were always sympathetic. Other men were often coarse and brutal, both in language and behaviour. My soul quietly rebelled. I hated nothing so much as filthy stories, but every boy must hear them. When I was in trouble or difficulty I always went to Master Bedford. He used to listen like a father to my story, give me good advice, and always finish, "Put up with it, my lad, till you know your trade." I saw this was a long and tedious process. Some of the men seemed to have an interest in keeping me back. A sort of custom prevailed that an apprentice should be kept to this kind of work the second year, and some other kind of work the third year, and the two last years sashes and frames, staircases, shop-fronts, handrails, and other advanced work, like a finishing school for ladies. I shall never forget the joy when a chalked board was placed on my bench with a full-sized drawing of a one and a half inch four-panelled door in section. It was my ambition to make this door as true as a hair, and in nearly the same time as a journeyman, but Master Bedford, who worked at the next bench, said, " Don't hurry over it. First learn to do your work well, no matter how long it takes, and then learn to do it quickly." When I finished the door it twisted, although I had taken the greatest care in planing up the framework. I fortunately discovered this before the door was glued up. I took it all to pieces in my own time, and found that the fault was in the mortices. The second time the door was a success, and I was proud at having turned out, from beginning to end, a good four-panelled door.

Every now and then there was a good deal of friction between me and my master and uncle. With either one or the other there was always something wrong. In my master I had to deal with one of the most violent and passionate of tempers. The most trifling incident or mistake would throw him into an outrageous temper ; he would swear, his lips and face turn red and blue, and would quiver like a leaf. I have seen him take off his hat and kick it, and after the storm ap-

peared all over he would return in a few
minutes and go over the performance again.
At first it was frightful, but I got accustomed to it. The men understood it, and in
winter-time never answered him, but in the
summer there were regular rows, with violent
threats on both sides, and three or four men
paid off at once. All this would arise from
using a piece of timber four by two and a
quarter instead of a four by two, a size not
in stock. My uncle had no visible temper.
He said cutting things, was cold, unimagina-
tive, fond of chopping down trees and making
everything ugly. He was philosophically
cruel without a drop of the milk of human
kindness in his nature. These two men were
my masters, and I never remember a week
passing without a collision with one or the
other—sometimes both. There were other
apprentices in the town, and we associated
together. They all sympathised with my lot,
and used to say, " Before you are out of your
time, you will be killed."

Some of my companions were what would
be called rabid teetotalers ; they believed that

drink was the upas-tree of our civilisation, and if people would only abstain the world would become a paradise, and every man would be a brother. Many of them were Methodists, and it was impossible for me to enjoy their company without becoming a teetotaler. For fourteen years not a drop of any intoxicating drink passed my lips ; but I was sent nightly to the " Rose and Crown " for the supper beer. My abstinence exposed me to the jeers and ridicule of the workmen, who used to speak of teetotalers as hypocrites, secret drinkers, liars, and gluttons. I was the only abstainer in the shop, and knowing all this to be false, I was often much pained ; but what hurt me most was a suggestion from Master Bedford that for my own comfort in the shop I should pay another footing and break the pledge. This social persecution only bound me more tightly to my party, and deepened my conviction of the evils of drink. I used to attend lectures by such men as Hocking, Grubb, Whitaker, Dr. Burns, Rev. Thomas Spencer, Cassell, Dr. Lees, and others. Some of these men I knew later on more intimately. I read all the

temperance literature and prize essays until
I had mastered the subject in all its details.
It became unconsciously the fanatical idea of
my life. But what great things have been
accomplished by fanatics bound together by
one idea, although the idea may not stand the
test of any philosophical inquiry! We were
not only moved by the same opinions, but we
were bound together in a common brotherhood, we helped one another. When I shook
hands with a teetotaler I felt towards him a
kind of heart communion.

During the winter about a dozen young
men formed themselves into a band of temperance pioneers. This exposed us to more
jeers and ridicule. We visited the neighbouring villages, sang temperance hymns, held
meetings in cottages, barns, and schoolrooms.
In time we attracted attention by the recla-
mation of some notorious drunkard, and if we
could arrange for some one to look after him,
bring him to meetings to relate his experience
and get him interested in the work, the recla-
mation of such a man was certain, especially if
his wife became a teetotaler. The most suc-

cessful and permanent conversions were those
in connection with some church, and in which
the habit had not been one of long standing.
I began to believe with my companions that
all efforts to improve the social life of the
working classes were hopeless except through
teetotalism, and a longer experience has not
materially altered that opinion. During the
winter we held meetings in villages, and I
have reason to know that these meetings
checked the drinking habits of the time, and
occasionally reclaimed a drunkard if he were
not the son of drunken parents. Whatever
little success I may have achieved in after
years as a public speaker or lecturer is due
to these meetings.

If I were not indoors by the time the
church clock chimed a quarter past nine
I was locked out for the night. On four
or five occasions before the clock had finished
chiming I could see as I entered the wicket
gate, when my footsteps must have been
heard on the pathway, the light suddenly
extinguished and the door locked. I now
walked the streets for two or three hours,

and then slept in the stable with rats; but as the man came about five o'clock to feed the horses I had to leave before his arrival. No one knew or cared where I slept so long as the shop door was unlocked at six. This kind of lodging was not very luxurious in the winter, but I had no money for any other, and I had to put up with it or give up attending meetings, which was what my master and uncle were determined I should do, and I was equally resolved not to do. It was my only pleasure, and the only time I had to enjoy the friendly intercourse of young men animated by the same thoughts and wishes. After much persuading and coaxing, a poor drunkard of the name of Jacob was induced to become a teetotaler. In a short time he was transformed into a respectable man. He joined the pioneer band and used to go with us to meetings. He had great natural gifts as a speaker, and his description of a drunkard's home and family was only surpassed by Gough. How could I leave the simple, impassioned language of this man to be indoors by a quarter-past nine? I used to

think if I had only his power I would go
through the country like Peter the Hermit,
and cry, " Down with the drunkeries ! "

At one of these meetings I made the
acquaintance of a young man who had lost
his father; this was a bond of sympathy.
He had descended from an old and respected
family of Friends, and was apprenticed to his
uncle, who was a miller and corn dealer. Our
ages were about the same, and our views on
most things were similar, and we seemed to
be gradually drawn closer to each other by
influences difficult to explain. I always felt
he was my superior in position and education;
he had read more and thought more. He
lived with his mother and sister in a pretty
cottage on the side of a small brook, which
was full of gudgeons and watercress. After
a pleasant walk across the fields one evening,
he said, " Mother wished me to ask you in to
supper." I accepted the invitation. The
mother had on a grey dress, a white silk shawl
over her shoulders, and the characteristic cap
of a Friend. She sat in quiet stateliness near
the window, which looked into a well-stocked,

old-fashioned garden. There was every sign
of cleanliness and order, but none of luxury,
although they were fairly wealthy. Presently
the door opened, and there entered a young
Quakeress, the sister of my friend. She was
about seventeen, of rather dark complexion,
full black eyes and black eyebrows, and hair
parted evenly over the forehead. She had
been in the garden, and was dressed in a grey
dress, with a woollen tippet as white as the
driven snow, which seemed to add additional
beauty to a face which I thought angelic. It
was a joy to look at her, but I wished I had
never seen her. She came to me and said,
"I am glad to see thee; I have often heard
my brother speak of thee, and I felt sorry for
thee, because thou hast no mother, and I have
no father." My heart burst into a glow, and
from that moment Rachel was my only
thought or hope of happiness in this world.
I was hungry, but ate little supper. My heart
was already too full, and when we gathered
round the table for reading and silent worship
my eyes and heart involuntarily wandered.
If there was anything in this world of tears

and sorrow which could give a moment of pure, heavenly pleasure, it was to look at Rachel. My admiration of her only made my attachment stronger to her brother; but I never mentioned her name to him. I began to think my love for her was wrong, and was the work of the evil one; but I could no more help it than I could help feeling hungry; and if, as I had read somewhere, all ethical laws should be based on natural laws, there was nothing wrong in my love for Rachel. I never mentioned her name to any one, but her form was ever present, and I could never shake her from my memory. I thought the better way was to avoid seeing her, and yet I always walked in the direction in which I expected to meet her. I kept up friendly relationships with Rachel's brother, and if I were again invited to supper I hoped to be able to make some excuse. In a few days I was invited, and I refused, for which I was afterwards sorry. I thought perhaps I should never again have the chance of refusing, and my foolishness made me unhappy. I endeavoured to find some comfort in the belief that she did not care for me and was ignorant of my care for her; but I thought from her behaviour and looks perhaps she *might* care for me. But Rachel had been comfortably and delicately brought up. She had been well educated; her condition and her prospects were good, for her father had died wealthy. How absurd for me, without much education or prospects, beyond a journeyman carpenter and joiner on a guinea a week, to think anything about Rachel; and yet I did think of her, for she belonged to a sect which valued labour above gold; I felt that a good trade and a virtuous life were worth something.

I knew she went to Sunday School every First-day, and if I walked in the opposite direction I might accidentally meet her, and perhaps her brother and mother, whom I was not anxious to meet. My Sundays were very different to what they used to be. I seldom went either to church or chapel, although I was bound by my indentures to go regularly to church. I occasionally went to Meeting, where I saw Rachel. Her mother asked me why I did not go to Meeting more regularly, instead of walking in the fields or by the side of the river. Some one complained of my Sabbath-breaking, and the lawyer who prepared my indentures sent for me and threatened me if I did not go to church or some place of worship. I proposed the Friends' Meeting-house, where Rachel went; but he objected—I must go to church.

What with selling shavings and doing little jobs in the evening, I managed to keep myself in pocket-money. One evening I went to a small china shop to put in a new sash-line. After I had finished the master asked, "What's the damage?" I replied, "Sixpence." He said, "You are the cheapest chap I ever employed." He gave me a shilling and asked me to remain for tea. We sat down, and his wife, a kind, good-natured Yorkshire woman, with whom you at once felt at peace and at home. There were several varieties of cakes, hot and cold. Over the chimney there was a long, straight sword with military trappings. The master saw my attention was drawn to these things, and said,

"I carried that sword through the battle of Waterloo with the First Life Guards." I began to feel I was now in society. He used very strong language about the Duke of Wellington for reducing his pension and increasing his own. It was always an exciting subject, and his wife used to say, "William, don't get so angry," to which he replied, "If I had what I ought to have there would be no occasion for us to keep this damned china shop." He quieted down for a few minutes, and then began cursing the Government and all its works. He asked me if I had read Burns's poems. I had never heard of them. He asked what I did on Sunday afternoons. I replied, if it was not wet or cold I went for a walk. He said, "Come down here next Sunday afternoon." I was rather glad, because he was so different from the men with whom I had to work. He could talk fluently on religion and politics, the Church, Paper money, Pitt, the war, George the Fourth, Reform, Sidmouth, Castlereagh, the Cato Street Conspiracy, James the Second, Hunt, and William Cobbet.

The following Sunday he received me with a pleasant smile, and in a few minutes brought out a large copy of Burns's poems, and after reading a verse or two, which he did with much feeling, he would stop sometimes in the middle of a verse, and say, "Now pay particular attention to what he says about the 'priests with hearts as black as any muck, and lawyers' tongues with lies turned inside out.' My God, how he hated the whole crew! I like him because he was a Radical." After about an hour I made a pretence of going, when he said, "You will remain for tea." Buttered toast, cake, cold roast pork—how delicious when you have no consciousness of a stomach! I was told to come every Sunday, or when I liked. As I was leaving he asked, "How do you get on with that gravy-eyed, psalm-smiting old Calvinist of an uncle?" I replied, "Middling." For some months I was pretty regular in my visits. I never made any remarks unless invited, because he disliked the comments of others. He read through most of the poems, and some of them two or three times, until, at last, I remem-

bered a good part of them. He now wished
me to hear him read another book, Paine's
"Rights of Man." This appeared to me a
very sensible sort of book, and as my host
made no secret of his opinions he had very
few friends. I was afraid Rachel would hear
of my visits, so I gradually broke off my
acquaintance, but not without regrets. I
thought I should like to have a copy of
Paine's "Rights of Man" to read secretly
at my leisure, and I asked a bookseller the
price. He replied, "I should like to give you
your rights with a horsewhip."

CHAPTER VI.

Leave my lodgings—Assist in establishing mechanics'
institute, which drifts into political club—Village
Politics—" No Dook shall Rain over us "—See
Rachel again—Speak lovingly to her—Imaginings—
Try to invent mortise machine and get kicked for my
pains—Run away—Get work at " the castle " —
Letter to Rachel miscarries—Parish constable arrests
me as runaway—A night in the cage—Am disgraced
by being before magistrates and put to rougher work
—Save money and join the Rechabites—Again run
away—Reach Saltbury—Get work—Help gentleman
build his own house—The drink again—The Chartist
agitation — Fall ill with small-pox — Nursed by a
gipsy.

I HAD now passed about three years of my
apprenticeship and began to feel more independent.   I could do as much of some kinds
of work as a man, and in day work at private
houses was charged as a man ; but I wanted

more leisure. In summer-time I often worked from five to eight, and during my apprenticeship my only holidays were Christmas Day and the day following. I now refused to come in at nine o'clock, and if I were locked out before half-past ten, I threatened to break the door open. This led to a row, and I was told to lodge elsewhere. I packed up my few things and lodged for a few days at the temperance coffee-house until I found a lodging with a whitesmith and his wife, who were Methodists and teetotalers. I was now more comfortable than I had been for some time. I soon found that my leaving was not liked, and although the days of dog-whips and bread and water and basket cords had passed, I had to submit to many indignities. I was put to the dirtiest and most unpleasant work, fit only for a labourer. While others were working under cover and in the warm places, I was sent out in the frost and snow to mortise oak posts too heavy for me to lift, and I had to move them as best I could. On Saturday I received seven-and-sixpence, and I was told this was the weekly wage for that year. I subsequently found that my wage was ten shillings, and so I was robbed weekly of half a crown, and if it had not been for occasional jobs after work I should have had a rather hard time. As it was, I could only afford butcher meat once or twice a week, but I could purchase good beef dripping at four-pence a pound as a substitute for butter.

An agitation was raised by a few of the leading artisans for a mechanics' institute. A room was taken over the market-place and opened three evenings a week. Books of all kinds were presented, most of them of a religious and disputative kind. The *Penny Magazine*, the *Penny Cyclopædia*, the *Mirror*, also *Dispatch*, and *Examiner* were taken in. Most of the mechanics in the town joined, beside a few shopkeepers and innkeepers. Scientific and literary lectures were occasionally given by itinerant lecturers. The genteel people would not attend lectures at a mechanics' institute, and they started a literary and scientific institution. It was a bad time for educational work. Bread was dear, trade was bad, and the country was passing through the

throes of a political convulsion which was fast
ripening into a revolution. The mechanics'
institute gradually degenerated into a violent
revolutionary club. The door was locked, the
passages watched, the most inflammatory and
seditious things were read and discussed, and
most of the men took an oath and swore if
there was a general rising they were to march
at once on the local bank. Collections were
frequent to meet the expenses of trials which
were taking place all over the country. One
of these meetings had been held far into the
night. The following morning found all the
shops closed and the militia on the pavement.
The men thought, as some believe now, that
salvation can only come by force ; but what is
gained by force must be held by force.

In a few months there was great rejoicing
because the Reform Bill had nearly passed.
Men believed then, as some do now, that all
our social and political grievances can be re-
dressed by changes of government; but when
all the resources of legislation are exhausted—
and we ought not to rest till they are exhausted — there will still remain questions

which no form of government can solve, and can only be solved by the individual reason and self-restraint. No excitement is so dangerous and seductive for a young man as political excitement; you drink in all the ill-will and hatred of those who differ from you, and unconsciously become a violent, hot-headed partisan. I had drifted a long way into this condition. The well-to-do people who were comfortably clothed and fed, who carried large prayer-books in the street, and went regularly to church, represented to my mind the wealthy supporters of privilege, the pension list, class legislation, and every abomination, against which every honest man ought to fight.

One day a placard was exposed which described the Duke of Cumberland as a human butcher, whose journey through Scotland could be tracked by arms, legs, and heads of un-offending men and women, who hung on trees by the road-sides through which his troops had passed. He was to be the future king of England! I was offered a shilling to write on the church gate, "No Dook of Cumberlan' shall rain over us." The next morning there

was a little conversation round the church
gate, and the old crier, with a wooden leg and
gold-braided coat and hat, perambulated the
town, offering a reward of ten shillings for
the discovery of the person who had written
inflammatory and seditious language on the
church gate. No one claimed the reward,
and after a few days the incident was forgotten. One evening Rachel's brother and I
went to a village Meeting, and in course of
conversation I told him how restless and reck-
less some of the men were in their language
about the Government, and I feared there was
trouble in the future. To my surprise he
rather sympathised with the men; he said,
"See what the Society of Friends have
suffered and still suffer." I was rather
pleased to hear this, because I thought
Rachel would probably think as he did, and
would not think the worse of me because I
had to work and associate with political
malcontents who swore vengeance against
the aristocracy and the Church. After the
Meeting Rachel's brother said, "Let us call
on friend Bailey and have some supper; my

sister is there on a visit." My heart throbbed as if it had no room to beat. I had not seen her for some time, but to be once more in the same room with Rachel was to forget all my trouble. There she was, sitting at the window, more lovely than ever. We walked in the garden together, and we preferred the most obscure paths. How slowly we walked, but how quickly the time passed! Her brother called out, " Are thou ready ?—I have been waiting this half-hour." I asked Rachel if I should come and meet her when she returned home any time after six. I said it was a lonely walk for her to take alone through fields and spinnies, and there were gipsies about returning from the races, who would follow her and want to tell her fortune. She readily assented. I then felt most uncomfortable, and I almost wished I had not offered to meet her. Rachel wished me not to come to the house, but wait one field off at the stile. When I saw her my heart moved from its proper place, and I felt that all the world was nothing to me. We dawdled backwards and forwards across field after field, and I had it in my mind to say something, but I had not the courage to say it. When we came to the last stile I said, "Let us sit here for a few minutes and watch the sunset." I looked into her black eyes, and said, "Rachel, if I were a Friend I should be very fond of you." She replied, "Why don't thou become a Friend, then I should be fond of thee." I now felt sufficient confidence to speak more freely. I told her my troubles and hardships. I had no mother, and at that her dark eyes filled, and mine followed her example.

But the manners, habit, and language of a Friend in a workshop would have exposed me to jeers and vulgar ridicule, although I thought if people were to exercise their own judgment the Friends had as good a Scriptural basis for their religion as any of the other sects, but the idea of becoming a Friend after four or five years of discipline would only add to a burden already too heavy to bear. We parted at the little gate which led to her house. Rachel said, "John, if ever thou art in any trouble, and we can help thee, let us know. My mother often inquires about thee." I began to think I had turned the corner; I might go regularly to Meeting for a few years and not adopt either the dress or language until after I was admitted a member, which I could defer to my own time. I could keep a watch on Rachel, and after I was admitted into the Society I should marry Rachel and be set up in business; and as the Friends in the neighbourhood were among the best customers of my master, I should certainly take most of the work away from him. As I was favourably known to many of them through my temperance work and working in their houses and selling shavings, I was anxious to continue their good opinion, because they were very influential. Things went on pretty much as usual, with constant friction and intermittent rows about the most trivial things, such as a screw too many or too few.

A rather heavy job of panelling came in for some alterations in an old manor-house. I could and ought to have done my share of the bench-work, but I was put into a shed to do all the mortising alone. After a few days I was unable to sit down, and it occurred to me that I could make a machine that could be worked standing. I mortised the handle of a chisel into a lever, which worked like the handle of a pump; it acted very badly, I could not get the core out, although mortising machines somewhat after my model are now common. I thought my master was miles away, but he suddenly made his appearance, knocked me off the mortising stool with his fist, and kicked me in the back and stomach. I protected myself as well as I could, but I was cut about the head and hands, and my shirt was stained with blood. He said, "Get off the premises, you white-livered thief, and never let me see your face again." I went to my lodging, and my landlady asked. "Who have you been fighting with?" For two or three days I remained indoors, when I saw in a newspaper that a few young carpenters were wanted for the Niger Expedition. I walked to London and back, to find that the vessels had sailed. I resolved not to go back to the shop if I could help it. I had only a few jobbing tools at my lodging, and these I thought were not suffi-cient to obtain work. Although I was in sore trouble, I did not see how Rachel or her mother could help me. When I met any of he men in the street they would jeeringly ask, "What about the mortising machine?" When the cuts and scratches on my head and face were healed, I put my few tools in order into a basket, and, with a few shillings in my pocket, I started at three o'clock one April morning, with a sore heart, to face the world. I hated what I had seen of London, and avoided every road that led to it. I much preferred the country. After walking a few miles I heard that there was plenty of work going on at the castle, about eight miles further on. About the middle of the day, after I had made myself presentable, I called on Mr. Bilby, who had the work in hand. There was not so much contracting as now, day-work was the common practice; and although it might be a little longer about, it was better done. Mr. Bilby asked what wages I wanted. I replied, I would rather leave that to him, he could judge what I was worth. I was afraid he would ask about my indentures, and where I worked last; but he finished by saying, "Be here at six to-morrow morning." I slept that night at a public-house, but as I did not drink I was not a welcome customer. I walked about the town, looking at the outside of the castle, and wondering whether it was a contract job. I examined some of the corner-stones to find out the names of architect or builder, but without success.

The next morning I was placed with a very good man, and we went off together to the castle. I saw there was the prospect of a long job; oak floors were to be relaid, partitions and doors taken down and reframed, and all this work in beautiful rooms with a beautiful prospect. I tried to make myself handy and useful. I asked the man with whom I worked if he knew of decent, comfortable lodgings. He replied, " We have no children, and I daresay my missus could put you up." I was now very comfortable, and began writing a letter to Rachel, explaining why I had suddenly left, but I deferred sending it for a few days. My companion, who was a very nice fellow, occasionally threw out in good-humour mysterious remarks, such as, " You must have been apprenticed when you were five"; to which I replied, "Is not some of this oak beautifully marked? I wonder how long it has been here? What fine workboxes it would make!"

On Saturday I was paid at the rate of eighteen shillings a week. When I counted the money there was five shillings in pence, tied up in a packet of brown paper, and thirteen in silver. I said, "I think there is some mistake; I am paid three shillings more than I expected." He replied, "If you are satisfied, I am." What pleasure there is in running your fingers through your first payment for work! One thing weighed heavily on my heart. I was anxious to write and ask Rachel's forgiveness, and tell her I went to Meeting on First-day and thought over my conduct, but I could not see that I had committed any sin which required forgiveness. I began another letter referring to the happy time when we sat on the stile together, but in my final letter, which never reached her, I omitted all allusion to the stile, because I was not certain as to her feeling towards me. After I had written and re-written a third letter—for all my spare time was occupied with letters—it occurred to me how was I to get it to Rachel. The post was out of the question, because I knew her mother took in all the letters. My only hope was through a friend, to whom I enclosed Rachel's letter, and asked him to convey it privately to her. But this creature had the same feelings towards Rachel as myself, and instead of giving my letter to her, he gave it to old Tenterhook, the parish constable. Day after day passed and I began to wonder why I had no answer to my letter. I imagined all sorts of things, and was very unhappy; and I thought, if the worst came to the worst, and Rachel was willing, we might with care live on eighteen shillings a week.

After I had been at work just over three weeks, I was returning to my lodgings one evening when old Tenterhook, whom I knew as the parish constable, touched me on the shoulder and said, " Now, my jockey, you will go with me." He took me to a little public-house in a side street—the one I slept at the first night. Old Tenterhook drank brandy and water, and smoked a long pipe. I never spoke to him. I felt alone, though with half a dozen others, smoking and jeering at my being nobbled. The cart was ready, and old Tenterhook was nearly drunk; he put on the handcuffs and chained one leg to the cart, and we drove by the castle into the West Road. We passed Rachel's house, I with a sore heart and old Tenterhook drunk. In a few minutes I was locked up for the night in the cage. This was a dreadful night; the stench was sickening. An iron grating, about six inches square, in a heavy iron door admitted the only light, and the place was about seven feet square, littered with dirty straw on a stone floor. The church clock chimed cheerfully, and I began to think it was the only thing in this world that was cheerful. How many times had I heard it, in joy when I sat on the stile with Rachel, in sorrow when I was measured for a coffin! Now there appeared nothing for me but perpetual sorrow. About two o'clock in the morning there was a great noise and swearing outside the cage. I could hear men on horseback, and presently the door opened, when Ted Stobs and Bill Walton were pushed in and locked up for highway robbery on the heath. The language of these men was dreadful—how they could easily have hacked his whistle. I crouched down in the corner to be out of their way. Two women came with a tin teapot full of hot gin and water; the spout was put through the grating of the door until the two men fell helplessly drunk on the floor and went to sleep. How welcome was the first ray of light through the iron grating, the glorious gift of God to the prisoner! About ten o'clock old Tenterhook and two or three others came and unlocked the door and handcuffed the prisoners. The magistrates sat in a room at the " Red Lion "; the chairman wore a large white beaver hat, white trousers and neck-cloth, and blue coat with gilt buttons. He was a fine-looking old gentleman; the other magistrates were Mr. Newgate, at whose house I had worked, and two parsons. I was brought in by old Tenterhook, and charged with absenting myself without lawful excuse, damaging the property of his master, &c., &c. The magistrates put their heads together and whispered to each other; this was a most anxious time for me, because I had no idea of the punishment it might be—for aught I knew transportation for life. The chairman lectured me on the duties of an apprentice, and referred me to the idle and industrious apprentice; but I was not charged with being idle, and as my master was willing to take me back because I could earn as much as a man, I was discharged. (Fifty-five years after I sat on the same bench as a magistrate.) If I had known the law of proceedings I could have made a good defence, but I don't suppose they would have listened to it. I left the court an outcast, the butt and jeer of the workmen and my companions. The woman with whom I formerly lodged hesitated about receiving me back; it was only another sixpence a week that made her consent, although she always gave me a good character. It was sufficient for most persons that I had been before the magistrates—the next thing was to be sent to prison.

With a heavy heart, after an absence of nearly a month, I resumed my apprenticeship.

I was now little more than a carpenter's labourer, carrying heavy baulks of timber for roofs and floors, put to rough, heavy fencing, and sent long distances to work. After my degradation my only hope was that I should never see Rachel: my future was a blank. She was sent to her relations at Finchester, and I never saw her again. My acquaintance with her brother grew cold, and soon ended. Poor Jacobs was my chief companion, and he traced in some mysterious way all my troubles to drink. There was something in it, because there is a kind of friendship or brotherhood among men of the same convictions or belief. My life now grew more wretched and miserable. I had lost Rachel, and her brother avoided me, and I resolved to make another start the first opportunity. The prospect of another three or four years was intolerable. Bullied and threatened by my master and uncle, and constantly accused of things of which I was innocent, was more than I could bear. I used to say to the men that when my apprenticeship was out I should try and get a place as ship's carpenter. I said this for a purpose. I had no knowledge of geography, but I could see at the mechanics' institute a map of England and a gazetteer. I knew it was useless to go a short distance, because I should be sure to be brought back by old Tenterhook, who knew the country for twenty miles round, so I determined on not less than a hundred miles, which would be equal to an emigration.

I began saving all my money from odd jobs and shavings. The money I received weekly from my uncle was barely sufficient to keep me, and was less than what I ought to have received. I began getting my tools together and putting them in order. I had joined the Rechabites, a kind of secret society with a password. They had lodges all over the country, and were bound by a solemn oath to give advice and assistance to any brother who had the last password and card of membership. I had a list of all the lodges and secretaries, but I had not settled in what direction I should start. The last winter I went to a night school to improve my writing and arithmetic. I began to feel my ignorance. I could always read fairly, and was fond of it,

and could write, so my teacher said, a decent
letter. The winter was exceptionally severe,
and I suffered from cold, because I was always
put to outdoor work. How I welcomed the
return of March and the gradual lengthening
of days, the first whisper of hope! One Sunday, about the middle of the month, I walked
five miles to a Friends' Meeting. Here I
thought over my scheme, and hoped that
the inner light which Rachel used to talk
to me about would guide me rightly—not as
to my running away, because I had already
settled that, but in what direction I should
run.

I found that Dorchester, Birmingham,
Gloucester, Norwich, and Worcester were
about the same distance. There were lodges
on the road to each of these places, but I had
never been more than thirty miles from the
Chilterns, and a journey of one hundred
miles into an unknown country required some
consideration. I could walk thirty miles a
day with a carpet-bag, but with a heavy
basket of tools I should be tracked, and
probably overtaken, by old Tenterhook on

horseback. I wrote to Brother Henwood, who lived about sixty miles on the road to Dorchester, to ask him to take charge of two baskets of tools until my arrival, as Brother Buckley would shortly be travelling in that direction in search of employment. I wrote not from the place I was living at, but a place some few miles distant. In March the password was changed and new cards of membership issued. Each member wrote his name on the card after the secretary, and I wrote John Buckley. The first Sunday in April I rose early and walked a roundabout road, with two baskets of tools, to the "Waggon and Horses," where the west country waggons put up. I saw my baskets safely in the waggon, and returned to my lodgings for breakfast.

I occupied a good part of the day in seeing how many things I could stuff into a carpet-bag. Some time before I had sold privately a few things, collected a few shillings owing for little jobs and shavings, and I made up my mind to start the next Sunday morning. I knew I should be missed on Monday morning, because there would be no one to unlock the shop, and I should be thirty miles away. I left a slip of paper, "Off to the Docks." I started with a doubtful heart. I imagined every person I met looked at me with a suspicious eye. My only hope was to keep on walking, although I was not quite certain of the road and was afraid to ask. By night I had travelled thirty-two miles, and slept at a little temperance coffee-house. The next morning I was very stiff and tired, but after a few miles' walk I felt all right. After ascending to the top of a steep hill there opened up before me a scene of great natural beauty. The sun appeared to have risen out of the immensity of space, and was gradually lighting up the horizon, a sea of purple and of gold. As far as the eye could stretch there was a vast expanse of flat country, with little villages clustered here and there, with church spires and red-tiled roofs, mills which turned with the wind, such as I had never seen before. Everything in nature was peaceful and happy, but my lot was one of fear. Every man I saw might be another Tenterhook in disguise.

I had travelled somewhat out of my road, and
it was not till Wednesday I arrived at Brother
Henwood's, where I had tea and remained
the night. In the evening I accompanied
him and two or three others to a village
temperance meeting. I was about leaving
the next morning, when Brother Henwood
said a Quaker gentleman, who was present
at the meeting last evening, would pay my
expenses and give me twenty-five shillings if I
would attend five meetings the following week.
The money was most acceptable, but I was
not more than sixty-five miles away, in a
wrong name. Was it safe? Was old Tenterhook looking after me at the Docks? Was
there any chance of his finding me? Would
they take the trouble? No one knew where
I was, and this was an out-of-the-way sort of
place. I accepted with much fear the five
village meetings, but I was every day in fear
of being arrested, perhaps at a meeting. I
spent nearly a fortnight at Flatover, but my
fear of arrest made me miserable. I sent
my tools and carpet-bag on to Saltbury. On
my arrival at Saltbury I went to the lodge,

and one of the Levites took me to a comfortable lodging. As I was very comfortable, and
ninety miles from old Tenterhook, I remained
nearly a week looking out for work. The
lodge paid my lodgings and allowed me five
shillings a week for a month. I thought of
returning to Flatover for a day, for the purpose of informing myself if any inquiries had
been made. I knew no one could send a
letter, because no one knew where I was,
and I had to make my inquiries cautiously.
It was some relief to find so far no one cared
about me. I returned to Saltbury, and after
a day or two I thought of moving on, but I
was rather pleased with the people, although
their manners and language were different from
that which I had been accustomed to, and I
had some difficulty in understanding country
people. It was springtime of the year, and
everything looked cheerful. I went to Meeting, and never in my experience felt such
peace. I reviewed my whole life, but the
future was hidden. I felt conscious of doing
many things I ought not to have done. I
had loved Rachel; I had run away; I had

tried to make a mortise machine; I had left word about the Docks for purpose of deceiving others; I had put down a stock lock for a mortise lock; but I had been so far protected, which might mean forgiveness. If I had followed up these impressions it would probably have influenced the whole course of my future life.

Just as I was about moving from Saltbury I heard there was a gentleman just outside the town building his own house and employing his own men. There was nothing about the building of an ordinary square house but what I understood, and as the foundations were just out of the ground, I knew the door frames, partitions, and floor joists would soon be wanted. A man much older than myself was waiting with the hope of obtaining work. In a few minutes the gentleman engaged both of us. The bricklayers and labourers were already at work. If I suited I was to have twenty shillings a week and my companion twenty-four. The gentleman said, " I have undertaken to build my own house for two reasons. I will have the work well

done, and I can, if I wish, make alterations.''
The most curious thing was there were no
plans, and as the work went on this was
enlarged and that was altered, according to
the owner's fancy, and I thought it a very
good way, if you could afford it. My companion was far from a teetotaler, and he used
to jeer about my being one—they were a
low, lying, hypocritical lot. I had heard all
this before I came to Saltbury. Every opportunity he was off to a near beershop, and so
long as we were on the ground floor no great
harm came of it. We worked together for
three weeks, and one very hot day we were
framing partitions, and he pressed me to go
and fetch him a quart of beer, and because I
refused he abused me and wanted to fight.
In the afternoon he was drunk. I put up
with his insults, and any good-natured suggestions from me about not giving way to
drink was met with abuse. A few days after
the gentleman for whom we worked met him
returning home drunk. As soon as he left
work, the remainder of the evening was spent
in a drink-shop, and what made the matter

worse was that he had a nice clean wife and
two pretty little children. On Saturday,
when we were all paid, the gentleman asked
me to remain. I was in terrible fear. I
thought perhaps I did not suit. But after
the men were paid he asked if I would come
and see him to-morrow (Sunday afternoon).
I called, and after a little general conversation he said, "I must make a change at the
building." My heart sank. I said, "I am
sorry, sir, if I have failed to give you satisfaction." He replied, "I am well satisfied
with you; but I want to speak to you on
other matters." I thought the worst had
come. Perhaps he had heard or found out
something to my disadvantage. He said, "I
believe you are one of those people who drink
nothing stronger than tea," which he thought
a wise resolution for a young man to take.
We went into the garden, where a sumptuous
tea was provided, and I was for the first time
in my life waited on by a man in livery, who
treated me with great respect. I was not
nearly so comfortable as if I had made my
own tea and toasted my own rasher on the

end of a lath. I felt this kind of thing was quite out of my line. After a few remarks, the gentleman said, "I have seen your companion much the worse for drink, and I must send him about his business. Do you think you could take charge of the carpenters' and joiners' work?" I replied I thought I could if I had two or three men with me, but I should like to select the men. I now knew a fair number of men in the trade, and if he would give me a day or two I would think it over and let him know. If I could find two or three teetotalers and good workmen, everything would be right; but good workmen were often drunkards. I heard of one good man three miles off, and I went to see him, and I saw at once by his work that he knew his trade, but I had no authority to engage him or mention the object of my visit. We held the same opinions on drink and politics, and this was a sufficient bond of friendship. I told him where I was at work, and he replied, "You have a drunken fellow for a mate. How do you get on with him?" The next day I told the gentleman that for twenty-five shillings a week I could find two or three good carpenters and joiners, and jointly we could undertake the whole responsibility of the work, and do it with credit to ourselves, and engage others as they were wanted. In a few days we were all Socialists, and everything went on smoothly and comfortably. We got the roof on and tiled before the heavy rains of autumn, and the work from ground floor to the attics was thorough and good, to the lead flashings round the chimneys. In one room we cut down the floor boards face downwards, and here we prepared all the sashes and frames, shutters, doors, and skirting boards, and this occupied us through a good part of the winter, which was one of bad trade and great political excitement.

Numbers of men were out of work, bread was dear, and the Chartist agitation was violently active. Copies of the *Northern Star* and other Chartist papers found their way into every workshop. Meetings were held almost every evening and on Sundays. Some of the speeches advocated physical force as the only remedy. This led the more cautious men to separate. Every association had its moral-force members and others who were for more violent action, until at last they were divided into two camps. The men with whom I worked were members of the moral-force association, but some defeat or unjust imprisonment inclined them in the opposite direction. I went to several of their meetings, and heard Fergus O'Connor, Dr. Taylor, Bronteere, O'Brien, Cooper, Dr. McDougal, and others. I signed their petition, but never joined the association; I preferred the society originated by Joseph Sturge, which had similar objects. I thought it wise not to take any part in politics, although the Five Points appeared to me just and reasonable, and since that time almost everybody seems to have come to the same opinion.

One evening, on returning to my lodgings, I felt a dull, heavy pain in my back, with frequent shiverings. I thought I had taken a severe cold. The next day I could scarcely stand, but I went to my work as usual. The gentleman for whom I worked saw I was ill, and sent me home in his trap. I went to bed.

My room was in the roof, and lighted by a small dormer window in the roof. I had a magnificent view over the downs. The following morning I was much worse, and in the evening they sent for a doctor, a young man just qualified, who had started a practice a few doors away. He examined me, looked at my chest, and said, " I think you have small-pox." I replied, " Never; my mother died with it, and I understood I had it at the same time, and no one has it twice." He said, " I will send you some medicine, and to-morrow morning I shall be able to speak more positively."

I had experienced many wretched nights, but this seemed the most wretched of all. I lay awake and thought this was a judgment on me for running away, and the idea of dying so young and buried in a wrong name, and no one to drop a tear over my grave, where no one cared for me, was sorrow beyond description. If old Tenterhook had found me and had me transported my sufferings could not have been greater. I thought of my evening walk with Rachel, and how my grandmother used to kiss me after prayers. I revolved these things in my mind till happily I became unconscious. The next morning the doctor said, " You have small-pox; you must keep quiet. I will send you some more medicine, and give instructions about your diet." I remained in bed about a fortnight, and I looked for the doctor twice a day as the visits of an angel. For hours and days I was alone in a nearly dark room. How I watched for the first ray of light in the morning through a chink in the window shutter! I could see the sun sink behind the hill, and then all was dark. Shall I sink and escape the fret and sorrow of life with no one to remember me? A few doors off there lived a family of gipsies who repaired umbrellas and made tin pots, and they heard of my sickness, but not before I was getting better. The woman came unasked, and cleaned my room and made everything comfortable. She washed me over with warm milk and water, and gave me some herb tea. I felt very grateful to this woman, and I met some of the family many years after at Ascot. She came every day and brought me beef-tea. She made another infusion of herbs, which had to be taken at sunset. The doctor now only came once in two or three days, so there was no rivalry, and I had ceased taking his medicine. I gradually got stronger, and in about a month I returned to my work. I was gratified to hear that the gentleman for whom I worked made frequent inquiries of the doctor. I had some money, and called on the gipsy to pay any expense she had incurred through my illness. She was angry at the idea of my paying her ; if she had only known when I was first taken ill she could have cured me with a herb which grows under a certain planet. I trembled at the prospect of a doctor's bill—all my savings would go, and when I called for it the doctor said, "You need not trouble, the bill is already paid, and I am under a promise not to say who paid it." I believe the gentleman for whom I worked paid the bill, and this made me more determined that, as far as I had the power, all the wood work in the house should be honest and good, and that better work should not be possible. The house was built to live in, and there it now stands, an example of what work should be. In twelve months the woodwork was finished and the house nearly ready for occupation, and then I began to look out for other work.

CHAPTER VII.

I COULD have found work at Saltbury, but I
was anxious to get away and return to my
proper name. I mentioned my intention to
the gentleman, who expressed his regret at my
leaving the place. He paid me and gave me
a five pound note—I had altogether nineteen
pounds—and an invitation to call on him if I
ever passed that way. I started with a waggon
westward, and said to the waggoner in the

hearing of others who were travelling that I was not well off, and I hoped he would take me cheaply. "If you can drive a little and help unload, I will take you to Wiverton, a distance of sixty miles, for three-and-sixpence. Wiverton had a population of eleven or twelve thousand, and above fifteen hundred men and women were employed in the lace and woollen factories. After one day and a night we came in sight of Wiverton. It was market-day, and there seemed to be great activity in the town, which had two or three large cloth mills. I went to a temperance house, and on giving the password I was admitted to the lodge. I now gave my proper name, after living for months under an assumed name. It was often a bitter regret that I was obliged for my own safety to adopt another name, but I believe under the circumstances Aristotle would have justified it. Deceit of any kind is always troublesome. You are obliged to be constantly on your guard, or some trifling incident may frustrate your design.

I fell in with a man who was in a small way of business, employing three or four men. He was a teetotaler, and rather a leading man in local affairs. He was respected by some and hated by others; he had a fair jobbing connection in the town and neighbourhood, and had the reputation of doing good work. I asked him if he could make room for me. He replied if I could wait a few days he thought he could. I waited about a week, and on Monday morning he gave me a bench. It was the custom for men to stamp their names on their tools, but I thought it safer, especially as the stamp would be made elsewhere, to have only my initials. My first job was a pair of folding doors for a shop front. At the next bench was my master; it was not thought improper for a master to work and associate with his men. The bench on the other side was occupied by a rather elderly man, and I could see he was a superior workman, and I willingly undertook the less important parts of the work, because I was not certain about some of the curves. I have seen him put on his tortoise-shell spectacles and look at a curved line with the affectionate interest of an artist. The master saw it, but he never swore at him or said,

" You have your hands in my pocket all the time you are looking at that line." The clock striking for dinner was often a secondary consideration with him, because he found pleasure in what he was trying to think out and work out. It was a joy to work with such a man, and his object was to turn out the best work, and when the job was finished we congratulated ourselves that there was no better work in the town. Years after I have gone a few miles out of the way to look at it. I believe it still remains, an example of sound, honest work, not done by contract. My employer was not of the jerry-builder species, and that was one reason why he had a small business, and confined himself exclusively to wood work. The evenings in summer by the side of the river were most enjoyable, but the long winter evenings were often dreary and uninteresting, unless you looked after companionship with persons not always desirable.

I had for some time read everything I could lay my hands on about the Corn Laws. I frequently had large packages of tracts from Manchester for gratuitous distribution. My first conviction was that bread should be the last thing taxed, and my next that neither the farmer nor the labourer were benefited by the tax. Protection to agriculture meant taking from somebody else for the purpose of increasing the rental of land. The object of Protection is to raise the price of the thing protected, or it is no use. Out of what fund is the increased price paid? There is but one fund, and that is the labour fund. The wages of farm labourers have never been decided by the price of wheat. These opinions were most unpopular in agricultural districts, but I defended them, and laid myself open to the charge of being an agitator, and setting class against class. One winter we had a good deal of alteration and repairs at an old country house a few miles from Wiverton, and I lodged in the village, and spent most of my evenings either attending temperance meetings or with the village shoemaker, whose shop was warm and comfortable. He was a good talker, and drew together a shopful of labourers, who smoked the filthiest of tobacco. He was a physical-force Chartist, and had

rather confused ideas about the Corn Laws,
and thought it would be just as easy to obtain
the Charter as the repeal of the Corn Laws;
but he was positive we should never obtain
either one or the other without a revolution,
and this is my little friend—drawing from
behind the curtain a pike.

The agitation for the repeal of the Corn
Laws had now become general. It need not
have been a party question, but it was forced
into being one by the Protectionists, who were
all Tories. If Lord John Russell's proposition
for an eight shillings' fixed duty had been
accepted by the Protectionists it would have
weakened the League, and probably deferred
the total repeal for many years. But they
were for a sliding scale, and said that eight
shillings a quarter on wheat was not enough,
and so they ended with no duty. I think I
mastered the whole question. I could repeat
from memory the imports and exports since
the passing of the first Corn Law in 1820,
the average price of corn each year, the wages
of the agricultural labourer, and the rent-roll
and acreage of the principal landowners.

I engaged the clubroom at the "Three Jolly Farmers," and delivered my first lecture on the Corn Laws, and after the lecture we formed an Anti-Corn Law Association. I visited other villages with the same result, and for the first time I had the misery of reading an editorial article in the local *Earwig* which described me as a young squirt, a pestilent agitator going into peaceful villages, stirring up strife and discontent, setting class against class; that I was a dirty, loathsome creature, and ought to be washed in a horse-pond. I read this over and over until I felt a kind of sea-sickness; it made me miserable both day and night. I had no idea that the man who edited the *Earwig* had the power of tormenting a fellow-creature who had no remedy. These were early days— worse things were to follow. But after a time these paragraphs lost their sting, especially when I knew the men who wrote them. I returned to Wiverton every Saturday, and found these paragraphs had been copied into the *Wiverton Mercury*. I thought the better way was to go to my master, and if he thought

these attacks would injure him in business I
had better leave. "Injure me!" he replied.
"Why, they have tried for years to injure me,
and some who left me on account of my
religion and politics have come back because I
endeavour to do honest work at a fair price."

On my return to Wiverton I formed an Anti-
Corn Law Association, and I was elected
secretary. We held meetings, and the
membership increased in three months to
nearly three hundred, but we had great difficulties with the Chartists. We were afraid to
hold public meetings, because they would
come down in all their strength and move
resolutions in favour of the Charter, protesting
that they were as good repealers as we were,
but the repeal of the Corn Laws was more a
manufacturers' question than a working
man's, and taking this view a few Chartists
unconsciously became Protectionists. The
association began to number among its
members some of the leading tradesmen
and a few persons of influence in the neighbourhood, and this made the Chartists more
aggressive. There was also an association in

Wiverton for the protection of native industry, which met on market days at the " Crown and Sceptre." The association was not very numerous, but highly respectable ; nearly all the parsons in the town and neighbourhood belonged to it, and it was rumoured that there would shortly be a lecture, and in a few days the town was placarded. I called our association together to see if we would take any action, or move a counter-resolution, or get up a discussion. After hurricanes of talk, in which every one knew best, it was agreed that we should go early to the meeting and take our seats close to the platform, and not express either approbation or disapprobation of anything. It is the highest philosophy to sit quietly at a public meeting and hear your friends slandered and the most deliberate falsehoods told about them, but what rankles most is to hear these things applauded by parsons and go uncontradicted.

No sooner were the doors opened than the Chartists swarmed in and took possession. The platform was fenced off, or it would have been occupied by Chartists. Early in the meeting the discordant noises and catcalls and whistling and invitations to " Flare up, old Josser ! " were the premonitory symptoms of a row. Presently the door at the back of the platform slightly opened to see if there was a full house. The chairman, who was a lord and a considerable landowner, was followed by five Church of England clergy-men, two or three fat farmers, lawyers, election agents, and other full - blown Tories and Protectionists. While they were arranging their bodies on the platform the most dismal yell went up, which was increased to thunder when some one hoisted two loaves on a pole, one about the size of a penny roll, the other exaggerated into the size of a lace pillow, which represented the Free Trade loaf. The chairman stood waving his hand and gesticulating, but no one could hear a word except something about fair play. " The Reverend Mr. Toby was asked for a song," " Does your mother know you are out ? " " Who's your hatter ? " " Flare up, old Jerusalem ! " (a playful reference to a gentleman who had proposed the cultivation of Jerusalem artichokes as a remedy for agricultural distress.)

These and other personal remarks kept the meeting in lively good-humour, interspersed with refrains from Chartist songs. One after the other made ineffectual attempts to speak. Some of the gentlemen on the platform began to retreat by the door they entered. One gentleman, with a white choker and large shirt-collar, shook his fist at the meeting and called out, " You are a set of damned ruffians and blackguards ! " A rush was immediately made for the platform, the railings were torn down, the men swarmed up the sides, and, after a brief hand-to-hand fight, took possession, and began singing " Rule, Britannia ! " when the meeting quieted down, a chairman was elected, and resolutions were unanimously passed in favour of the People's Charter. The town, having nothing else to do, became excited, and the meeting had greatly intensified party strife. The following morning the chairman of the Protection to the Native Industry meeting was walking down the street when a shoemaker went up to him in the most polite manner, touched his hat, and said, "I beg your pardon, but are you the gentleman they calls Lord Dumpling?" He replied, "Yes." "Then," said the shoemaker, "I shall do myself the honour of kicking your behind." But, as this was done without his lordship's consent, the shoemaker had committed an assault, and some of the gentlemen had the satisfaction, a few days after, of giving him a month on the treadmill.

I urged the members of the Anti-Corn Law Association to keep free from all disturbances, and we issued a notice expressing regret at what had occurred, for which we were in no way responsible. At the same time we were willing to discuss the question in a friendly spirit, and if such discussion could be arranged, admission to be by ticket, one-half distributed by the Protection to Native Industry Association, the other half by the Anti - Corn Law Association. Some such arrangement appeared necessary to prevent the meeting from becoming a second edition of what had already taken place. After some time, Mr. Pipkin, one of the paid lecturers of the Protection to Native Industries Association, accepted the invitation. I wrote to ask Mr. James Acland to meet him. It was thought advisable to have one of the Anti-Corn Law lecturers. When everything was arranged a borough election began, and Mr. Acland was unable to keep his engagement. It was useless to make any proposal for postponing the discussion—this would have been a victory for our opponents. I was requested, as the lawyers say, to appear for the Anti-Corn Law party. I felt it a compliment.

I had acquired some confidence and command of language in speaking and lecturing; but I had an idea that other qualities were wanted in a discussion—some knowledge of logic—and if my opponent had this knowledge he might obtain an unfair advantage. I purchased a sixpenny book on logic, and if I had studied it so as to understand it my case would have been hopeless. I heard that Mr. Pipkin, who was to be my opponent, was to lecture at a farmers' club a few miles from Wiverton, and if I could manage to see him and hear him I should be better able to judge of my prospects.

He was more than twice my age and weight, but the latter was of no importance. I sat with a friend in an obscure part of the room, while the farmers smoked their pipes and drank hot brandy and water, and applauded such profound remarks as, " I have come here to speak to you," " I wish you well," " the enemy is in the field." And then followed the old worn-out platitudes about dependence on our natural enemies for food lowering wages; the inability of the farmer to pay his labourers; encouragement to home industries by import duties; sending gold out of the country to pay for corn, with violent attacks on the cupidity of manufacturers and the employment of babies in factories. Such was the staple of the lecture.

There was nothing in the lecture to frighten me; happily Bimetallism, Individualism, and Reciprocity were not born. I could see without logic that many things he said had no connection with the subject, and were only intended to divert attention. Bold assertions were made without any facts or evidence to support them—dismal prophecies about land

going out of cultivation and becoming value-
less ; landowners, farmers, and labourers,
emigrating by thousands. I thought if this
is the stock-in-trade of the Protection to
Native Industry Association, there was nothing
to fear from Mr. Pipkin ; but there was one
thing I did fear, and that was a very seductive
voice. It is not always what a man says that
carries the meeting, but how he says it. As
the evening for discussion drew near I began
to feel more uncomfortable. I called on the
secretary of the Chartist Association, and
asked him to use his influence to prevent any
disturbance. He said, " We are as strongly
opposed to the Corn Laws as you are ; they
are the natural outcome of class legislation,
which we mean to destroy. The middle
classes have obtained the franchise through
our help, and we are left to fight our own
battle. Your agitation is supported by the
wealth of the middle classes, and we are
obliged to fight you because the capitalists
are as much our enemies as the landowners."
I replied, " My sympathies go strongly with
you, but this discussion has been forced on

me. I am a young man, and I did hope for your friendly assistance." He replied, " Do you think you are strong enough for old Pipkin ? " I replied, " Yes, if I have fair play." " But," he added, " if old Pipkin is likely to get the better of you, hold up your thumb and we can break up the meeting."

The tickets were all taken in two days, and a large number were somehow distributed among the Chartists, and some were forged. The chairman was agreed upon. I never lost an hour's work, but for a day or two my limbs moved mechanically, with the prospect of this discussion before me. No statesman could ever have been more deeply impressed than I was with the injustice of the Corn Laws. To manage yourself is often more difficult than managing your subject. We came on the platform together, and my heart went into my boots. I felt nervous. We were received like two gladiators, with cheers and groans. Mr. Pipkin was in evening dress, with half an acre of shirt front. He had a large watch-chain strong enough to hold a bulldog, and from a ring there sparkled something white about the size of a pea. It is the worst possible taste to go before an audience of working men on any subject in dress boots, lavender kids, and diamonds. In the Sunday clothes of a decent mechanic, I felt more at ease than Mr. Pipkin. The chairman opened the proceedings fairly. He made a few remarks about getting at the truth, however disagreeable, and fair play for both sides, inclining favourably towards the young man. This made me more nervous, and the audience cheered. Mr. Pipkin led off about our dependence on foreigners. I had the whole thing at my fingers' ends. I asked where Mr. Pipkin's shirt came from, his gold chain, his silk waistcoat, and umbrella, and his beaver hat? His trousers and coat were probably made from foreign wool. Let Mr. Pipkin strip himself and stand on this platform, if he is not ashamed, as a man independent of foreigners. I could see I had made a point. We were at it from seven till ten, and more than two-thirds of the meeting voted for the total and unconditional repeal of the Corn Laws, and a petition to that effect was adopted by the meeting. As soon as I was in the street, they took me on their shoulders to the hotel; but as I was a teetotaler, and very tired, I excused myself from going inside. This unexpected demonstration would have been the ruin of some young men; it might have been my ruin but for total abstinence. As I walked through the streets the people used to say, " That's the young fellow who tackled old Pipkin"; and the labourers used to speak of me as a corn speaker. For some days I was rather a distinguished person, but distinctions soon pass away.

Soon after this demonstration my master took a three months' job about ten miles from Wiverton; and as he and one man were sufficient for home work, he sent me and two men to Marley Hall. We loaded a cart with material and tools, and started early in the morning. My companions were born in Wiverton, and they told me stories of small tradesmen and shopkeepers who had been persecuted and ruined on account of their politics or religion, or both; and if the Corn Laws were repealed these persecutions would go on at every election until we had the ballot. When I was ordered to Marley Hall my master could see that the proposal was not agreeable. I wanted to remain with the people with whom I had acquired fame. I wanted to gratify a vanity which has been the ruin of hundreds, and might have been my ruin had I not been sent to Marley Hall. I remonstrated mildly against being sent; but as my master had twice raised my wages without asking, I thought it better not to allow his wishes to be the cause of any difference between us; a trifling difference may soon grow into ill-will and hatred. On our arrival at Marley Hall we found lodgings in the village difficult to obtain, except at the "Marley Arms," where tramps, hawkers, and all sorts of persons lodged in a kind of casual ward, attached to the main building by a passage at the top of the staircase. Neither of us liked the prospect, and when the landlord found I was a teetotaler he could not possibly accommodate me. He could find comfortable beds for two. I knew what that meant. I went all over the village in search of a lodging, and the nearest approach was at a small farmhouse; they had a spare bed, but no bedroom. I slept comfortably enough on a truss of clean straw in the granary.

It occurred to me that as they had no use for the bed, I might have it, and take up my residence in one of the numerous dressing-rooms at Marley Hall, and save my lodging allowance. I could see by the furniture that these people had seen better days, and, to my astonishment, the woman said I might have the use of the bed as long as I wanted it; but she did not think it safe to sleep at the Hall alone —no one had slept there since the murder. I made a kind of bedstead with floor-boards; but sleeping in your clothes is far from comfortable. Just as I finished tea a lad came from his missus with blankets, sheets, pillow, and horse-cloth. I now had the prospect of a comfortable bed in a lonely house. Marley Hall had not been inhabited for forty years. It was a long, rambling, Jacobean building, added to at different times without much reference to the original style. It had the reputation of being the scene of many horrid murders and battles. The last occupier hanged himself in the drawing-room, and his wife, on hearing of the suicide, jumped from her bedroom window into the moat, and was drowned. Ghosts held nightly revels in Marley Hall. Every person in the neighbour-hood had seen them, jumping out of closed windows and back again without breaking the glass. Some had been seen with knives and swords stained with blood, others carrying bleeding heads on pikes, dancing on the grave-stones of the neighbouring churchyard. I was glad not to have heard this ghastly his-tory before going into residence.

The first night I heard no noises, such as doors opening and shutting, but once or twice I heard distinct tappings at the window, whether from the inside or outside I could not deter-mine. I remember when a boy at Claywick, where we had one or two ghosts, and that if I was ever disturbed by one I was to cross myself and say boldly, " In the name of the Father, the Son, and the Holy Ghost, why troublest thou me ? " I was rather glad when the morning light began to shine in countless

needles through chinks in the window shutters.
I again heard the tapping at the window, and
thought it rather late for ghosts to be out. I
dressed myself and sat on the bed, but though
I could see no ghost, I heard it tapping; I
began to think there was something in ghosts.
Over my bedroom was another similar window,
by the side of which ran a stackpipe fastened
to the wall by a strip of leather which had done
duty as a driving-rein. It had rotted off the nail
on one side, it hung loosely from the other nail,
and was so sensitive that the slightest breath
of wind caused it to vibrate and strike against
the glass of the upper window. I could have
sworn with a clear conscience that the window tapped was the one in the dressing-room.
Having found out one ghost I took no further
trouble about the others, but slept comfortably
amid the screeching of owls, the creaking of
doors, and the nightly procession of rats.
When the men came to work I said nothing
about the ghosts, because I knew they would
only make fun of me.

The first day or two we walked about the
house and grounds, and looked over the plans,

to get some idea of the alterations marked blue. We agreed that three months without help would never see the work finished. We began tearing up floors, taking down partitions and ceilings of rooms that were to be heightened, in which we were assisted by labourers from the village, who were useful in bringing up provisions. Our cooking was rather primitive —a fryingpan, saucepan, and teakettle ; but with these we managed, with a good digestion, to live pretty comfortably.

The master visited us once or twice a week and brought us the newspapers and provisions. The men went home every other Saturday, but on Sunday I generally dined at the farm on boiled pork or bacon and parsnips and hard dumplings, price fourpence. On the return of the men on Sunday night or Monday morning I heard all the news of Wiverton. The Chartists had become more violent and demonstrative ; two or three had been arrested. They went to missionary meetings and Bible meetings, and passed resolutions in favour of the Charter. They held large open-air meetings on Sundays, obtained the use of an old chapel, where sermons were preached and Chartist hymns sung. Lectures on Peterloo, the Bristol riots, the Monmouth rising, and the Pension List were common. Bad trade, low wages, and dear bread were the stimulating causes of a widespread discontentment. Men were driven to their lowest depth of hatred of the governing classes. To keep me from this danger and excitement, which my master foresaw was coming on, was his chief reason for sending me to Marley Hall. Spies gave evidence as to what they had heard at meetings. Some of the leaders were imprisoned and tried at the assizes, and unjustly, as some believed, punished. Although the Chartists were divided into sections on matters of action, they were united against privilege, pensions, and class legislation. They were mostly without votes, but their influence at elections was always with the candidate farthest on the road. The man in favour of one point was preferred to the man against all the points, and this was how they won point after point until they gained almost all they asked; and by this time the other two points would have been gained had they not been split up and weakened by divisions among themselves, occasionally fomented and encouraged by their enemies.

The working classes were never so united or powerful on any political question as on the Charter, and probably will never be so united again until some great and good man shall arise who is capable of combining the discordant elements in favour of one or two well-defined objects. Unless the working classes drink less and strive for a higher political morality they must be content to bear disappointments and remain where they are, with less power than they had before their enfranchisement. The first Reform Bill, Catholic Emancipation, the abolition of Church rates, the repeal of the Test and Corporation Acts, and all the civil and religious liberty we enjoy, took a century of agitation. Public opinion cannot be manipulated like a telegraph, men will not learn that evolution in sociology and politics, as in the natural world, is a slow-developing process.

Nearly the whole summer was spent at

Marley Hall, and I began to notice a marked change for the worse in one of my companions. Evening after evening in the taproom and skittle alley of the "Marley Arms" began to tell its tale. The desire and excuse for drink became more frequent, until at last he was often fuddled at his work, and was in time, after frequent warnings, sent about his business. The landlord of the "Marley Arms" who had taken his money, expressed no sorrow, but it was a warning to others.

One bright September the sun shone out in all its splendour on Marley Hall. Everything looked lovely. The red bricks and stone mullions glowed with colour; the inside smelt of size and paint; the marbling and varnishing had now made Marley Hall habitable, and some thought beautiful. A screw here, a door eased there, and the job was finished. We collected our tools and set our face homewards with a cheerful heart.

CHAPTER VIII.

Changes—Wiverton elects me delegate to London conference—The corn leaders I met there—Dan O'Connell
compliments me on my speech—Sidney Smith and I
to make descent on agricultural counties—A Whig
gentleman—Meeting at Hockey—Polesfield and the
Olive despotism—Chased into a cottage and then
escape—Find a friend at Dighurst—I begin to attack
the landlords in over-zeal—Experiences—At Grundle
played only a garden engine—First glimpse of the
sea—Partnership with a missioner—Refused town
hall at Detworth—A publican farmer takes pity on
me and puts up tent in his paddock—Story of a placard—Have a grand meeting—Thoughts on my career
as an agitator—Further meetings.

IN a few months great changes had taken
place at Wiverton. The Anti-Corn Law
Association was nearly dead. The life of
these associations depends on the constant
activity of one or two men. The Chartists,
under persecution and suffering, had grown

more numerous, more bitter, and more un-
manageable. It is difficult for a young man
with political aspirations not to be drawn into
the whirlpool which first flatters him and
then destroys him. I at once set to work to
revive the Anti-Corn Law Association. Thousands of tracts and pamphlets and speeches
and Anti-Corn Law catechisms were distributed by house-to-house visits. In rural
districts the whole force of the landed aristocracy was against the League. A lying
and corrupt local press, often subsidised by
Protectionists, was scurrilous and libellous on
the leaders of the movement. Coarse, vulgar
caricatures were circulated among the poor
and illiterate, and these were worse than the
newspapers, which many were unable to read.

Towards the close of the year all the local
associations were invited to send delegates to
a conference which was to be held at the
Crown and Anchor Tavern in the Strand.
The meeting of Parliament was the time fixed
for the conference, and I was unanimously
chosen delegate, and as trade was rather slack
I offered no objection, but was rather pleased.

The little fame I had acquired by my contest with Pipkin had gone before me, and on my arrival in London I made off in hot haste, asking every few yards for the Crown and Anchor Tavern. I felt it most important that I should be there as soon as the doors opened, and I was bursting with all sorts of ideas and information which the conference ought to know, none of which I had any opportunity of laying before it. The conference lasted a week. We walked in procession, four deep, through an avenue of policemen, to the House of Commons with petitions for the total and immediate repeal of the Corn Laws. The police jostled us about more than was necessary, and prevented us entering the lobby, but the members took in the petitions. I never thought much of petitions; they involved an enormous amount of trouble and produced no result. Public meetings were held every evening during the week of conference. I had my first opportunity the third day, and my practical knowledge of agricultural life gave me a great advantage over cotton spinners. I could speak from personal knowledge of the condition of a Dorsetshire labourer. At these meetings I met Daniel O'Connell, Mr. Ward, Mr. Villiers, Mr. Milner Gibson, Mr. Bright, Dr. Bowring, Colonel Thompson, George Thompson, Mr. P. A. Taylor, Francis Place, Mr. Rawson, and Mr. Fox. I kept up an occasional acquaintance with Mr. Cobden and Mr. Bright until the dark veil separated us. I came up with Mr. Cobden from Petersfield on his last visit to London, and a few weeks after I attended his funeral. I shall never forget the sorrow of Mr. Bright. The last day of the conference we all dined together at the Palace Yard Hotel for two shillings and sixpence each. I sat between Daniel O'Connell and Mr. Fox, and made another speech which I knew—and you can always tell—to be a good one. Anyhow, Daniel O'Connell shook me by the hand and paid me a compliment! The *Morning Adver-tiser* and *Chronicle*, and I think the *Times*, wrote short articles on my speech, which appeared to give general satisfaction. I received a letter from my master to say trade was still dull, and I need not hurry back, but there was work when I returned. I gave the letter to Mr. Rawson and Mr. Paulton, who showed it to Mr. Sidney Smith, who was secretary to the Metropolitan Anti-Corn Law Association, and it was arranged that I should remain in London and attend meetings. I went first to the Green Gate Tavern, somewhere in St. Luke's; the landlord presided. Nearly all the meetings in the metropolis were held in public-houses. Fifteen miles round London was worked in this way. New Associations were formed and old ones revived and encouraged. The life was not to my liking, and yet there was something fascinating about it. No one knows the pleasure there is in publicly denouncing a wrong or injustice unless they have experienced it.

As soon as the winter was over it was arranged that Sidney Smith and myself should make a descent on the agricultural counties. I was to go first and find out if a room could be obtained, whether the Protectionist feeling was strong, and whether there was likely to be a row. I had the names of a few tradesmen in each place who were supposed to be favourable, but when I called on them they did not like to be seen speaking to me, and often discouraged me from attempting a meeting, although they were in full sympathy with the object. Occasionally I called on some Whig gentleman who lived a few miles from the town, with a view to his taking an interest. He sometimes had the undeserved reputation of being a good Liberal. I toiled up the hill full of hope. I thought the influence of a man who lived in a large house surrounded by a park must be all-powerful in the district. I never dressed in the first style of fashion, and I had a great contempt for "mashers." I rang the bell, when a man gorgeous in laced livery made his appearance, and, before I had time to speak, said, " Go to the back door." I stood a minute thinking where I ought to go. I had a general letter of introduction signed by the chairman of the League, when a head came out of the window. " What do you want? " I apologised, and told him my business and gave him my letter. He said, " I can take no part in any meeting. I think the Anti-Corn League ought to be suppressed—it is going too far in attacking the landowners. I am for a fixed duty." Now this man a few months before had unsuccessfully contested a place in the Free Trade interest, and his expenses had been paid by the League. His son was engaged to be married to the daughter of a neighbouring landowner, who was the militant chairman of a Protectionist association. I walked back to Hockey and resolved never to call again on any man, favourable or unfavourable. In future they should come to me.

On my arrival at Hockey I found a bellman who agreed to cry the meeting (which I intended to hold) three times for five shillings. I stipulated that the times should be when the men were going to dinner, when they left off work, and half an hour before the meeting. "O Yes! O Yes! O Yes! This is to give notice that a lecture on the Bread Tax will be delivered this evening at seven o'clock, at the open space behind the town hall. Working men and their wives and all persons are invited. God save the Queen!" I followed the crier at a distance to see he did his duty—his last round was rather groggy. I always took a position, if possible, with my back against a wall; a barrow for the platform, or a stool or chair could always be had for sixpence. I had a strong voice, and found no difficulty in speaking to large audiences in the open air. Occasionally a few men of the baser sort would try to make a disturbance, which could generally be traced to a public-house. I finished by saying if they wished to hear more of the subject—and they generally did— and a suitable room could be obtained, a gentleman from London would come and speak to them. The next morning I made arrangements for Sidney Smith's lecture. My meeting had created an interest and was preparatory to his visit, which would often create the greatest excitement and enthusiasm in a sleepy agricultural town.

I went on from Hockey to Polesfield. I found there was no place of accommodation but the "Olive Arms." I sent round the crier, and while I was having my tea I could see knots of persons gathering towards the square. Tradesmen came out and talked anxiously to their neighbours, and there was a little commotion among them. The landlord came into the room where I had just finished tea, and said, with adjectives not worth writing, that "one of them Manchester agitators was in the town, and he hoped they'd make it 'ot for him." The place, body and soul, had belonged to the Olives since the Flood. The church appears to have been built to put up lying tablets to their memory, which told you not what they were but what they should have been. The Olives had represented the place undisputed since the Saxon Heptarchy. The Olives were the chief landowners. The Olives were everybody, and everybody had to be for the Olives. A meeting against the Corn Laws was one of the most impudent and insulting things ever attempted in the land of the Olives.

As the hour drew near my heart began to sink. I was a stranger alone in a strange place. I stood on a step under an equestrian statue to one of the Olives, with my back against the railings, and in a rather nervous, desponding tone of voice I asked them to hear what I had to say. I at once saw a few sympathised with me and were anxious to give me a hearing,

but the agent of the Olives came and ordered
me off. I had no right there—the market-
place was the property of the Olives, and if I
refused to go the police should remove me. A
man called out, "Come into my garden." The
crowd, which was now large, moved towards the
garden, but a few half-drunken fellows, with the
steward at their head, prevented their entrance.
I sent a lad for my carpet-bag, which had been
thrown into the street, and I took refuge in a
labourer's cottage. His wife was frightened
and very angry, and talked excitedly about being
turned out and ruined like old Cutler the
Chartist. I could see from the prints on the
wall of John Wesley preaching from his
mother's grave, and his escape from the fire
at Epworth, that these people were Methodists,
and at that time all the Methodists were Liberals
and Free Traders. Presently I heard the breaking of windows and cries of " Turn him out ! "
The lad brought my bag to the back door.
The man said, " Now you make off in such a
direction across the fields towards Dighurst,
and I can say you have left the town." I
started off, hiding myself as well as I could by

the side of hedges and trees. Fortunately it was getting dark, and this helped me. I came at last into a road outside the town, and overtook a labourer who was going to Dighurst. My companion had come from a neighbouring village and knew nothing about Polesfield. I had some difficulty in understanding his dialect, but I found out he had a wife and large family on a wage of ten shillings a week, and bread tenpence a loaf. And this was the man for whom the Olives wanted Protection! My indignation rose to fever heat, and although I was never for physical force, nothing would have given me so much joy as to have marched on Polesfield with an army of agricultural labourers and wiped out the Olives.

On our arrival at Dighurst I did not forget my companion. There is no man on earth so good as a simple, trustful, agricultural labourer, uncontaminated with the filth and greed of thickly populated towns. I found a comfortable lodging at Dighurst in a house near the church, and after a basin of bread and milk went to bed, but not to sleep. The events of the past few hours oppressed me; we were

living under a social tyranny more cruel than
the worst of despotisms.   In the morning I
looked round the place and walked in the deer
park and had a look at the castle.   I fixed on
a place for the meeting, and sent round the
bellman, and just as I was sitting down to a
boiled sheep's head and dumplings a man
came to my lodgings and asked if I was the
person going to lecture, and I replied "Yes."
"Pack up and come and remain with me while
you are in this neighbourhood."   Here was a
man not afraid of territorial magnates.   His
wife received me kindly, and at once set out the
dinner; there were no apologies for having
nothing to eat.   She said, "I am glad you
have come; we can make you comfortable if
you will only make yourself at home, which is
sometimes difficult.   We want a little en-
lightenment in these parts.   Our man has just
come in from Polesfield and told me of the
treatment you received last night.   If we had
known we could have sent for you."   In the
afternoon her husband drove over to Polesfield
and remunerated the man for the damage done
to his cottage.   Nearly all the front windows

were broken, the door split, and his fowls let out. The mob went into the place, and when they found I was not there they retired to the different public-houses to celebrate their victory. The police offered no resistance to the mob or protection to me. Summonses would have been of no use; they would have been heard by a Protectionist bench and dismissed with costs, and this would only have kept up the excitement and ill-feeling. A few persons wished me to return, but the local newspaper recommended a horse-pond.

To my conviction of the injustice of the Corn Laws, which was deepening every day, there was now added, what I had carefully avoided, a dislike of the men who supported them, and for the first time I began to attack the landowners and ask by what right they monopolised the land which was given by God for the use of all? What right had they to enclose commons, shut up footpaths, add the land by the side of roads to their fields, pull down cottages, take possession of all wastes, and persecute to helplessness and poverty every man who resisted them? This exposed some, with me show of reason, to the charge of setting class against class, but it was the strong burglar class against the poor and defenceless.

Towards seven o'clock the men began to assemble for the open-air meeting. The great local man, who had lost his estate by gambling, was living abroad; what remained of his estate was in the hands of Jew moneylenders and lawyers, and his castle was occupied by a stockbroker, so he was rather at a discount with the people. The tenants were rack-rented, the labourers had lost their commons and were badly paid, and in winter many were out of work and lived partly on charity. A waggon was drawn up by the side of a wall with a large open space in front. Agricultural labourers and their wives were present in large numbers, and the waggon was occupied with speakers and newspaper men. The gentleman who entertained me took the chair. Then followed two or three labourers, whom I knew were local preachers by their language and dependence on the Lord for the repeal of the Corn Laws.

I remained at Dighurst for a fortnight, holding open-air meetings in the neighbouring villages. On two or three occasions the church parsons offered a little opposition, but they certainly met with no encouragement from the labourers. A farmer would sometimes grunt out some question, such as, "Ain't you paid to come here?" I generally replied by saying, "If you are not paid to come, it is very silly of you to be here. I should have remained at home to feed the pigs," when some one would call out, "He ain't got none, and only about half a dozen ship!" It was the only way you could deal with these men; they had neither the knowledge nor sense to argue. Their politics and religion came from the landlords and the parsons; one told them what a jolly thing it was to be a farmer, the other to be content. I met with a good deal of kindness from the labourers' wives. I occasionally went to tea with them, but how could I eat and drink what the family wanted without paying? I have seen in some obscure cottage, with the ever present companions of poverty and sorrow,

self-denial and true heroism, far nobler than
anything that can be observed in the houses
of the wealthy and the great.

I now moved on to Grundle, which also
sent a farmer's friend to Parliament, and in
an open space at the end of the town began
my address. I could see there was trouble
ahead. A few well-dressed blackguards in
white trousers and hats, smoking cigars and
singing, came rollicking down the street, and
at once began to interrupt and push the
people about. They brought out a garden
engine, and I was squirted until I had scarcely
a dry thread left. It was fortunately very hot
weather, and my clothes soon dried. I saw
some of the men were getting excited, and
began fighting. I walked through a park in
the direction of Fogmoor; it was now dark,
and I put up at a little inn. I was hungry
and tired, and ate a crab with my tea. No
words can describe the agony of that night,
and from that day to this I have never tasted
a crab. The next morning, for the first time,
I saw the sea. As wave after wave rolled up
tons of pebbles like chaff, I felt how feeble a

creature man is among the forces of nature.
I was softened and subdued by the grandeur
of the sea, which seemed unfathomable, restless, and eternal. I found there was a mission
going on every evening which attracted crowds
of persons, and I feared this would interfere
with my meeting. I sought the missioner, a
type of creature not to my taste, brim full of
Scripture texts. I explained my object, but
he had a far nobler object beyond the sky.
It had been given to him to preach the glad
tidings of great joy, the blood of our Lord
Jesus Christ, and Him crucified. I replied I
did not pretend that cheap bread would save
people's souls, but it might do good to their
bodies, and our objects were similar, only his
was the higher of the two. I asked how he
got on for expenses. He replied, "Rather
badly—the collection last evening was only
two-and-fourpence." I could see he was open
for business. I said, "If I give you half a
sovereign will you shorten your service, and
mention that you do so to oblige a gentleman
who is anxious to speak on another subject?"
He agreed. The meeting was on the beach,

and in the course of the evening three hundred had signed a petition for the repeal of the Corn Laws.

Three evenings I went into Christian partnership with the missioner, and I think I was growing the more popular, and to avoid any unpleasantness, because I could see he did not like his spiritual business to be less thought of than the bread that perisheth, I now moved on to Finchester and addressed a meeting from the steps of the market cross. Finchester was under the protection of a Tory duke, who could send his sons into Parliament to represent the borough without a contest. It was useless to attempt any opposition to the dependants of a duke. No one, except a few labourers, dared to be seen at a Free Trade meeting. A few shopkeepers stood at their doors within hearing distance, with playful smiles on their countenances. The landlord of the "Badwood Arms" brought out a chair and a glass of brandy and water and smoked his pipe in peace. I spoke loud enough for them all to hear—for hearing depends upon the atmosphere. I asked why they did not come nearer, and was told that if asked, as they might be, by some of their customers if they attended the meeting they could say " No " with a clear conscience. My efforts to obtain a room for Mr. Sidney Smith failed. I tried hard for the British school, but the managers were afraid to lend it. I now started for Detworth. Here the town hall, market-place, and almost every house and inch of ground belonged to the lord of the manor, who represented the borough. He lived in a large house just outside the town. I was advised to ask him for the use of the town hall, which was rarely refused for any useful object. I walked through the park and had a full view of the house. I was satisfied no Free Trader lived there. I saw a man sweeping the path, and asked if Mr. Grindham was at home. He replied, " That's un going in." I hurried up, and when he saw me he waited at the front door. I asked him if I could have the town hall for a meeting. He replied, " Yes, if you pay the hall-keeper five shillings." I thanked him, and hurried off as fast as possible ; but the man I saw sweeping I could hear was

running after me, and I had to return. I now
entered the great hall of Detworth House,
hung with portraits of kings and queens and
ancient Grindhams in armour. Mr. Grindham asked what sort of meeting I wanted.
I replied, "A Corn Law meeting." After a
few other questions he discovered my object;
he had given permission for the hall under a
misapprehension. He thought I was some
missionary or conjurer, but he now found I
was one of those paid agitators that went
about the country setting the farmers against
their landlords and the labourers against both.
No meeting of the kind should be held in
Detworth. I thought of returning to Dighurst, which was only a few miles distant.
I called at a little inn just on the borders of
the town to have tea. The landlady, a nice,
clean, comely woman, said, "You don't look
well, you had better have a little brandy in
your tea." Presently the husband came in,
a farmer-looking man, and we soon fell into
conversation. I soon found out that he hated
the Grindhams with a perfect hatred. They
had robbed the parish of the common, and

his father of a cottage and two acres of land, and refused to subscribe to the labourers' sick fund so long as the meetings were held in his house.   He was the only Liberal in the place, and that was why nearly everybody avoided him.   He had two cows and a few acres of his own, which was as much as he and his wife could manage, and if the Grindhams were to offer him ten times the value of his land they should not have it.   They had tried two or three times in an underhand sort of way to buy it.   As he was a farmer I was in doubt as to how he felt on the Corn Law question, but after a little judicious heckling I found he was a friend of my friend at Dighurst, and that he was a Free Trader.   I now spoke more freely, and related my recent interview with Mr. Grindham.   He said, "It was no friend who sent you to him.   Are you the young man who was at Dighurst the other day?"   I replied, "Yes."   "Ah! I could not get over that evening; but if you will come here next week, that paddock is mine," pointing to a little field, "and I will have a tent put up and two strong fellows at the gate to keep out the Grindham lot. I'll get the trap ready, and we will drive over to Dighurst and arrange for the meeting. The printer at Detworth would be afraid to print the bills; he lives in one of Grindham's houses, and at election times makes a good thing of it.

The drawing up of the bill, a copy of which I kept for several years, was more difficult than drafting some Acts of Parliament. My farmer friend was a fighter; he wanted the bill headed, " Another gross act of tyranny by the Grindhams! The landlords defied! Great victory over feudalism! How long are we to groan and suffer under the despotism of landlords? " But I objected to my name being on such a bill, and it would be objected to by the League. After much talk better influences prevailed, and the bill was at last printed with a full headline, " A Challenge to the Land-owners! As no other place can be obtained in Detworth, a public meeting in favour of the total abolition of the Corn Laws will be held in Mr. Fallow's paddock," &c.

As I walked alone through the meadows I began to think how much happier I should

have been if I had kept to my trade and
never meddled with these questions. Here
I was a wanderer on the face of the earth,
with no fixed home, no future, disowned
by relations and friends because of my
opinions. Except the helpless, the poor, and
the defenceless, every man's hand seemed to be
against me; but it was now too late to turn
back. The poverty-stricken condition of the
labourer, the ignorance and selfishness of his
employer, the utter absence of all humanity
or sympathy with his struggle for existence
against what appeared to be hopeless conditions, supported me and comforted me with
the belief that I was doing a religious work,
as holy in the sight of God as any missionary.
To see families of a bold peasantry, their
country's pride, reduced to living for days on
bread and turnip-tops, gathered by permission,
was enough to drive men to acts of violence.
How could the repeal of any law make their
condition worse ? The only things which the
greed and malice of the rich had not taken
from the labourer were the pure air and sun-
shine of heaven, the glorious colours of a

sunrise, the budding hopes of spring, the tints of autumn, and the song of birds. Surrounded by these free gifts of nature, he returns home after the labour of the day to eat the taxed bread of misery and sorrow, to swell the income of the landowners.

My friend from Dighurst started early with a few others for the Detworth meeting. On the road we passed a number of labourers and their wives and babies on their way to the meeting. From a little elevation we saw men in batches coming across fields and footpaths towards Detworth; others were driving along in carts. On our arrival we were received with a welcome which must have been heard at Grindham House. Here and there we saw a policeman, some of them taking notes; they had a peculiar self-satisfied expression which only policemen can put on at political demonstration not acceptable to the gentlemen of the quarter sessions. The tent would not accommodate a tithe of the crowd, and waggons were drawn up at different points and occupied with speakers, and that most dreadful variety of our species, newspaper men. When everything was quiet my farmer friend said: "My brothers and sisters, let us commence this meeting by asking the blessing of God, and singing a verse or two of a hymn." The meeting reminded me of a great camp meeting of Methodists. After a short prayer for the conversion of the landlords and farmers, he gave out, in a powerful voice—

> "Who is this gigantic foe
> That proudly stalks along,
> Overlooks the crowd below
> In brazen armour strong?"

The whole affair was pathetic because it was toned with religious feeling. My farmer friend reviewed what had taken place in his father's time and his own time. The farmers and the labourers had gone from bad to worse —no wood for the ovens, no commons for the geese, and no labourer allowed to keep fowls or a pig, or glean. Several labourers spoke, and said all their wages were spent in rent and bread. A petition for the repeal of the Corn Laws was unanimously adopted to Parliament, signed by the chairman and forwarded for presentation.

I returned to the London centre, which is
now a large postal and telegraph office. I
reported to the secretary the places I had
visited, with a diary, and gave the names and
addresses of persons with whom he could cor-
respond. We now arranged for a tour in two
other counties. I arrived at Chalkover, which
sent a Protectionist to Parliament, early in the
day, and sent the bellman round and gathered
together a large audience. I remarked that the
people were more free and buoyant when the
place was not owned by one man. Chalkover was
the centre of a large agricultural district with
a number of small villages a few miles distant,
and I arranged for a meeting in each of these
villages. The first parish I visited the parson invited me to tea. This was such an unexpected incident that I was almost afraid to
accept it. I found he was not exactly a Free
Trader, but a High Churchman with large
sympathies with the labourer. I was far more
at home speaking to a hundred labourers on
the village green than to larger audiences in
towns. The Wesleyans and Primitive Methodists helped with names into other villages.

The secretary would never speak at open-air meetings, so he kept to the towns where rooms could be had, and I kept to villages, but my meetings largely helped the town meetings, because I used to announce at my village meetings the town meetings. After about three weeks I moved on, taking villages and sometimes towns on my way to the west. These meetings were pretty much alike.

CHAPTER IX.

IN five weeks from the time I left London, with a meeting somewhere almost every evening, I arrived at Barne. Here the people gave me an enthusiastic reception. I addressed a large audience from the balcony of the "Ramsdown Arms." The secretary held a meeting in the assembly room belonging to the inn, where the member for Barne presided. I began to think that public opinion on the Corn Laws was not the result of any reading or thinking, but a kind of compliment to the person who had most influence in the place. No Protectionist could have been returned for Barne, nor could any Repealer have been returned for Gippham—a borough a few miles off—which sent Protectionists to Parliament, and had been represented by members of the same family for a century. A meeting here appeared hopeless, and as there was no bell-man, I began speaking in a wide, open space near the church. A policeman came up and said he had orders from the mayor to move me. The audience resented this, but it was of no avail. One man called out: " Let us go outside the borough ! " And from a heap of limestone by the side of the road I spoke to a large audience which was incensed by the action of the police. I begged of the men to go home and have no altercation with the police, or they would get into trouble. Every person known as a Free Trader in Gippham was regarded as a sort of burglar who wanted to divide the land and confiscate the property of the rich, and destroy the con-stitution, whatever that might be. This was

the kind of language recently addressed to the
farmers at their annual show. After visiting
a few villages, avoiding those in favour of
saving the constitution, I went to Balborough,
a place which sent a strong Protectionist to
Parliament. I was anxious to arrange a meeting here for the secretary. The only room was
one in connection with an inn which was let
to conjurors, comic singers, and Bible meetings. I saw the landlord and engaged the
room, for which I paid ten shillings, and went
to the printer's with a draft of the bill. I
could see at once there was something wrong.
The printer stroked his beard and asked,
" Are you sure you have the landlord's permission for this meeting ? " I replied, " Here
is the receipt, and I want the bills out at
once." He asked me to call again in ten
minutes, but the landlord and printer were
both after me. The landlord swore, threw
the half-sovereign at me, and said: " No
man in Balborough would be such a big
fool as to give any encouragement for an
Anti-Corn Law meeting." I at once started
for Barne, and on my road at the outskirts

I saw a cobbler's shop with a copy of the
Northern Star in the window. This was a
sufficient introduction. I began by inquiring
the nearest road to Barne, and we gradually
fell into conversation. I inquired if the
Northern Star had much of a circulation in
Balborough. He replied, " I believe mine is
the only copy, and I have to go four miles for
it." I asked if I might look at it. " Certainly " ; and he swept a seat for me with his
leather apron. I saw there was a violent
article against the Anti-Corn Law League ;
I expressed my regret that Chartists should
be so opposed to the abolition of a tax on
bread. He replied, " Give us the Charter,
and we will take off the tax ; and we can
get the Charter as easily as you can get the
repeal of the Corn Laws. Look at this place—
all Tories and Protectionists. I am avoided
like a leper. Look at your House of Commons and your House of Lords, made up of
landlords, or men sent there to protect the
interest of landlords who sit in the House
of Lords. They will never repeal the Corn
Laws without a revolution, and I don't care

how soon it comes. I have my machine ready
in the back kitchen." We had tea together,
and I told him the object of my visit to Balborough, what had taken place, and my failure
to secure a room. He said, "I wish you could
have a meeting, because these landlords want
showing up; the farmers and people about
here think they are little god almighties, and
are afraid to say anything or do anything for
fear of offending them. We have just had
a Ranter's chapel built, where they occasionally have lectures. You might get that
if you saw the superintendent, who lives in
a cottage next the chapel—it is just out of the
town, but that would not matter." "Now
if I should succeed, will you promise not to
come and disturb the meeting?" "There will
be no occasion for me to come. The chaw-
bacons and lawyers and flunkies and hangers-
on at the house will do that." I went to the
cottage of the superintendent-preacher of the
Primitive Methodists, a small, square house
like a packing-case, which was built with the
chapel. It had a small parlour and a kitchen
downstairs, and two rooms and a cupboard

upstairs. The walls were whitewashed, and the staircase was entered by a door in the kitchen. His wife, neat and clean, in a cotton dress and white cap with a frill, sat knitting stockings, and on the table was an open Bible. The furniture of the kitchen, where they appeared to live, consisted of four wooden chairs and a deal table. On two shelves over the window were about a dozen religious books and the minutes of Conference. I began by congratulating the minister on the new chapel. "Yes," said he, "the Lord has been very good to us poor folk; we have had to endure much opposition and persecution in this place, but, thank the Lord, we have at last, through prayer, triumphed. The chapel will hold two hundred, and the people who come are mostly agricultural labourers and their families; they built the chapel." "But," I said, "I thought the agricultural labourers in these parts were badly off?" "They *are* badly off. I go out and preach five evenings a week in labourers' cottages, and I know they have often not enough to eat." "How, then, could they build the chapel?" "One man gave us some bricks, another some wood, and I went begging. The members gave their labour, and used to work in summer till it was quite dark, and we have only a debt of about seventy pounds on the chapel and house, and the interest is paid out of my stipend, which is sixty pounds a year. Some of the members agreed to give twopence a week towards paying off the debt, but I knew they were often without bread or coals in winter and were unable to keep up their payments, and I never asked them." Finding our sympathies with the condition of the labourer were mutual, I gave a sovereign towards the chapel debt. "Thank the Lord, O my soul!" said the minister, and his wife responded, "Amen; the Lord prosper Thy servant." He asked me to kneel down for a few minutes' prayer. As soon as we stood up the minister, turning to his wife, said, "I told you good luck was coming to-day; I saw a ringdove on the chapel roof this morning."

I now introduced the object of my visit to Balborough. I said, "In villages I have met with much encouragement from your people.

I have shown them that the Corn Laws
not only made their bread dear and wages
low, but were opposed to all Christian teaching." I then asked for the use of the chapel
for a gentleman to give a lecture on the
subject. I could see there was some doubt
on his mind. He said there was something
settled at the last Conference about allowing
chapels for political meetings. He took
from the shelf the minutes of the Primitive
Methodist Conference, and there it was stated
that in future chapels were not to be used
for political meetings. I said that minute
had special reference to Chartists' meetings,
which were often noisy, and some of their
ministers were Chartists, and had been pro-
secuted and imprisoned for using seditious
language in their chapels. I said a lecture on
the anti-Scriptural character of the Corn
Laws was no more political than a lecture on
the wanderings of the Children of Israel or
the travels of St. Paul, and if the Corn Laws
had been in existence when Jesus Christ was
on earth He would have preached against
them.

I mentioned the names of several prominent Primitives who were repealers, but the minister said he should like to consult one or two others. I began to think the investment of a sovereign was premature. As I was leaving the place, I said I should like an answer at once. His wife was evidently favourable, but as I had experienced the result of consulting others, I rather pressed for a decision. His wife dropped her knitting, and, as she began warming the teapot, said, "William, why don't you send the boy down to Bill Lapston? He once belonged to us, and knows all about the Conference minutes, and he studies these things more than you do." Presently Bill Lapston made his appearance, and, to my fear and astonishment, it was the shoemaker. I looked at him with an expression which he understood, and when the minister had explained the object of my visit, asked what he should do, and read the minute of Conference, which Bill Lapston knew as well as he did, to my delight he replied, " Have the lecture ; it can do no harm. And if they pull down the chapel the League would build another; they had plenty of money." I laughed, and said that was his fun, and I gave Bill Lapston another look. Fortunately he expected a customer, and could not wait for tea. Everything was arranged, but the minister was anxious to give a religious tone to the business, without which, he said, the meeting would not succeed.

Now the secretary, who was to lecture, was a Unitarian, and I had no idea what he would think of the following programme of the meeting : Commence with singing and a short prayer; lecture to be delivered from the pulpit; the bill announcing the lecture to have a headline, " And all nations went into Egypt to buy corn "; the lecture to be free. I felt it most desirable to attack this strong Protectionist fortress, and if the secretary had any scruples about conditions, then I would ascend the pulpit. I have often lectured from the pulpits in Scotland. In taking leave of the minister I advised him to begin the singing and prayer punctually at seven; and as we had a drive of some miles and the roads were heavy, we might be a little late.

I called on Bill Lapston and thanked him for his help. He said, "I knew by your look what you meant when I came into the room." I offered him half a crown for his loss of time, which he indignantly refused. He said, "If I had a wife and family wanting bread I would never take a bribe." I was sorry he had taken it in that light, and we parted good friends. On my arrival at home I explained everything to the secretary, who at first was not favourable to what was a new departure in announcing the meeting, but we settled the draft of the posters, and sent a man over to stick them. In the interim the secretary visited some of the neighbouring towns, and I went to the villages.

We had an early tea, and started for Balborough so as to arrive about just after the singing and prayer. As we neared the chapel we could see all along the street a great commotion, and as we came nearer we could hear the loud singing. The secretary turned to me and said, "I almost wish you had taken this meeting." When we drove up to the door the excitement was intense; cheer after cheer outside and the singing inside only increased it. The chapel was packed, and numbers outside, unable to obtain admission, listened eagerly at the door and windows. We went into the little cottage and had a cup of bad tea. The minister had caused the lecture to be advertised through the circuit, and the congregation had been waiting and was growing impatient. We entered a little side door, and the secretary went straight into the pulpit, and was received with deafening cheers. I sat with the minister and his wife and three or four local preachers. As soon as the applause ceased the secretary began, " I come from a country that made the notable discovery three hundred years ago that religion did not consist in a heap of consecrated bricks and mortar, but in the sacrifice of a humble, penitent, and obedient heart" (followed by audible "amens" and " Bless the Lord ! " from every part of the chapel). " I know of no place," he continued, " more suitable for pleading the poor man's cause than this place, which can be truly called the poor man's church." The meeting lasted nearly two hours, and was from beginning to end most enthusiastic ; and this was the commencement of an attack which continued till the election and the return of a Free Trader to Parliament.

The Council of the League had now resolved to contest every place without regard to any hope of success. It was not long before bye-elections offered an opportunity. In manufacturing districts elections were comparatively safe and easy, but in small agricultural boroughs, where farmers spent their money with tradespeople, and one or two lawyers had managed to get the affairs of the corporation into their hands, the contest was by no means easy or certain. The struggle went on for weeks, and during that time there was little or no business, except at the public-houses, and as the final day drew near the excitement increased. Every public-house window had a placard, " The committee sit here daily." Then there was a liberal circulation of electioneering literature on both sides, sometimes personal and scurrilous. The central committee,

which often consisted of a man and a boy,
was besieged from morning to night with a
seedy, dilapidated, red-nosed lot of fellows
who wanted to be employed as canvassers,
runners, clerks, scouts, messengers, watchers,
and poets. One had enormous influence with
farmers, another with tradesmen, another
with Freemen, and one or two had influence
with the clergy. If you declined to avail
yourself of this powerful influence, sufficient
to win a dozen elections, then, much against
their principles, they would all go over to the
other side.

The constituency of Arlingford was about
three hundred. The candidates had issued
their addresses, and it was some days before
they appeared before the free and independent
electors. The Farmers' Friend was a feeble
lot. He talked about the Constitution,
Church, and State, protection to native
industry, and something about the Malt
tax, but his lack of oratory was made up by
the most boisterous manifestations of applause
from his supporters, who cheered and hurrahed
every word. Our candidate was a good

speaker, and he made an excellent impression on the non-electors and some of the more thoughtful electors who were free to vote. Speechifying, drinking, bill-sticking, and canvassing were in full swing; and from the canvassing books—for, against, neutral, doubtful—there appeared some chance at least of a close contest. Put not your trust in canvassing books! The men canvassing on both sides used to meet at a public-house and arrange their books. The only trustworthy canvass was that voluntarily made by the candidates and their friends a few days before the election. The opposition started a procession with flags and band, which used to march round and hurrah at the committee rooms of the Farmers' Friend and grunt and yell at his opponent's, to keep up both sides of the equation. A Free Trade band and procession was organised, and it required good generalship to prevent the processions meeting. For the first few evenings this was arranged by both processions marching the same route; the blue was to start twenty minutes before the orange. The evening before the nomination, by some mistake or wrong order, like the Balaclava Charge, the Free Trade procession entered one end of the narrow street, and a few minutes after a Protectionist procession entered the other, and ought to have retired. Yells of "Go back!" and "Go forward!" proceeded from both parties, but neither party was disposed to go back. As they came nearer they slowed a little, and the big drums were pounded at the rate of sixty miles an hour, and a collision was inevitable. The bystanders held their breath. The more sensible on both sides ran away, but there was a sufficient number left to fight who were either too fat or too drunk to run. Happily they had no sticks, and it is wonderful what a lot of pummelling can be done with the fists without serious injury, and they were too thickly packed to fall down. Rush after rush was made for the flags, which were taken and re-taken. The drums were broken, and the drummers defended themselves with drumsticks. But what added to the row was a number of women who had come for their husbands. Some of them fought better than the men, and were encouraged by the hurrahs of opposing parties, and "Go it, Sal—give it him!" to a poor fellow helplessly wedged in a doorway until his face was scratched and punched almost beyond recognition. At last both sides appeared to have had enough; and a cry that Tim Belcher and two others were killed damped their political ardour, and after a battle of thirty minutes the little street was nearly deserted. Early next morning a few free and independent electors visited the scene of battle. The shutters and doors were smeared with blood and dirt. The pavement was stained with drops of blood which had been shed for and against the constitution. Remnants of blue and orange ribbons were scattered about with scraps of union jacks and remnants of clothes and buttons. The municipal scavengers were early on the scene, and by breakfast time all traces of the battle were wiped out, except in the scratched faces, black eyes, and swollen lips met with in the streets.

The nomination was to take place the following day, and both sides were for vengeance. But it passed off quietly, because both parties were equally balanced and too much exhausted to renew the fight. They were only able to yell, and throw rotten eggs, dead rats, and other garbage at the candidates. A bugler was engaged by the Tory party to lead on, and he had never failed them till now. The excuse was that he was so hurt in the wind at the last night's fight that he was unable to blow. The show of hands was in favour of the Free Trader, and for a few hours our candidate was member for Arlingford. The polling next day reversed the decision of the day before. The poll was declared every hour, and for the first few hours we had a small majority. At one o'clock we were six behind, and at four we lost by twenty-three. The Tory Farmers' Friend was returned! The Free Trader and most of his friends left before the close of the poll. I remained behind with a clerk for a few days to settle the accounts. Nearly five weeks had been occupied in swearing, lying, drinking, fighting, and speechifying, and during this time much sin and wicked-

ness of a worst kind was committed. Law-
suits between relations and friends sprang up,
and hatred in many cases became permanent.
The streets still rang with " Rule Britannia "
and " God save the Queen," and this was how
the constitution was saved in the hour of
great peril. The chairing of the member was
the last act in the pantomime of a free and
independent election. Early in the morning
ladies were to be seen at every window
elegantly dressed with a profusion of blue
ribbons. They carried large bouquets to be
thrown at the Farmers' Friend as he passed.
The member was single, and this made the
hearts of all the ladies, especially the single
ones, flutter with delight.

Early in the morning one of the scouts
came to my lodgings. He had a profound
secret to communicate. He said, " There will
be some fun at the chairing to-day. Twenty
or thirty chaps met in Cooper's barn last night
and swore they would upset the chair ; and
a lot are coming from Henson to revenge
themselves for the fight in Jenkin Street."
At about eleven o'clock the chair, decorated

with ribbons and flowers, followed with a band, and a procession dotted with black eyes and bruised faces and swollen noses, carrying flags, marched to the town hall, where the member was in waiting with his committee. Some time elapsed before the member made his appearance, and the news went round that something was wrong, and the chairing would not take place for another hour, perhaps put off altogether. A good many left, but others went and refreshed themselves freely at the public-houses. The attacking party kept out of sight. Presently a waggon was drawn up to the town hall. The horses were profusely decorated with ribbons and flowers, and a kind of triumphal arch had been erected in the waggon, and a floral chair placed under it for the member. There were other chairs for old Mortagee, the lawyer and agent, and a few friends. There was great anxiety and inquiry in the crowd as to the change of route. Some said the member had been taken suddenly ill, and Dr. Parsley had been sent for; others that the carriers were too drunk. Some of the committee had an inkling of what was likely to happen. The procession moved slowly off from the market-place to the tune, " See the conquering hero comes," and was expected to return in about an hour and a half. The ladies were very excited, bouquet after bouquet fell into the waggon, until it looked like a funeral. When the procession began to return everything was as pleasant as could be wished, and all fear of an attack had now passed away, because the procession had been through the streets where an attack was most expected. When the procession arrived at old Mortagee's house it stopped to hurrah. Ladies' heads were at every window like bunches of turnips. A little to the rear of the house and on the opposite side was a pair of heavy folding gates, which opened into an unoccupied stable yard, separated from a road at the back by a paddock. Access into the yard was across the paddock. One of the gates had a door by which stablemen and others entered. This door opened into the street. Three or four men rushed out and climbed into the waggon. While the gentlemen were bowing and kissing

their hands to the ladies they were attacked
in the flank and rear. A struggle and a fight
with sticks, fists, and umbrellas took place.
The ladies screamed. The man was ordered
to drive on, instead of which he turned half
round and blocked the street, which cut off
all help. He said he didn't hear; but others
said he was bribed, and did it to prevent any
assistance. The attacking party was quickly
reinforced by others who came from the road
in the rear through the stable yard. The
member, old Mortagee, and the committee
were defeated, and the member and two of
his committee were left in the waggon with
the only clothing, except boots and stockings,
they brought into the world. The ladies
retired from the windows shocked. The
naked were charitably clothed with great-
coats and rugs and quickly made their way
into old Mortagee's house. The victors
paraded the streets with two frilled shirts
on poles; and so ended an election at which
almost every elector hoped for something
besides a shirt. At the next election, a few
years after, the candidate had to be protected

from the sheriffs' officers. Old Mortagee and the Jews had devoured him, and slowly digested him like a boa constrictor. The man who for ten years had the borough at his feet retired to an almshouse, on six shillings a week, to make way for another of old Mortagee's nominees.

I walked alone to the station, which was a few miles distant, and gladly took my ticket for London, and in a few days started for my village lectures; but in a fortnight I was hurried off to another election, which I abhorred.

CHAPTER X.

ON my arrival at Salsify I found our opponents were in residence. The streets and houses were placarded with " Vote for Muggins, the tried Friend of the Farmer and Labourer." There were two large inns in the place: one in possession of the Reds

(Protectionists), and the other occupied with
the Yellows (Free Traders). The Whigs and
Tories had alternately represented the place,
by small majorities, since the first Reform
Bill, and there was a general impression that
the man who had the longest purse always
won. There were the usual speeches and
pamphlets, flags, bands, and processions, and
occasional street rows and fights. An extract
of some law about bribery and intimidation
was liberally circulated, but it had as much
influence on the purity of election as the
transit of Venus. The canvass books—such
as were honestly made up—showed a large
return of small shopkeepers and others who
had not quite made up their minds, and they
said nothing which gave you any idea what
their opinions were—if they had any. We
knew what this meant. Mr. Cobden, Mr.
Rawson, and others protested against the
illegal expenditure of sixpence. Mr. Cobden
said the legal expenses of the contest
ought not to exceed one hundred and fifty
or two hundred pounds, and if it exceeded
that sum it was not honestly spent. It was

observed that the friendly interviews between the electors and Mr. Birdlime, the Reds' agent, were becoming more confidential and frequent as the election drew nearer. The worry and anxiety began to tell, and for two or three days before the election the agent was confined to his bedroom, only making his appearance for an hour or two in the middle of the day in a Bath chair, when he was followed by a little party that had not quite made up their minds. As nothing could be had from our side, it was a common report that their principles might be all right, but they were a poor, beggarly lot, not able to pay for a pot of beer.

The anxiety about the health of Mr. Birdlime was most touching. The men who had not quite made up their minds, to the number of about fifty, used to visit him in his bedroom at all hours; but his illness was of so serious a nature that he could only see each one privately, and there were strict orders that only one person was to be admitted at the same time. Mr. Birdlime's bedroom had an inner and an outer door;

the inner door was covered with red baize,
which made it impossible to hear the conversation when both doors were closed. Everybody suspected what was going on inside.
The result of the election was settled in
Mr. Birdlime's bedroom.

Two or three days before the election a
commercial traveller appeared with his samples,
and took up his quarters at the inn occupied
by Mr. Birdlime. He complained bitterly that
all business was at a standstill through the
election.

He went in and out with his samples,
and told everybody he had not taken a line.
After the first night he wanted his bedroom
changed for one which looked into the street.
Now Mr. Birdlime's room looked into the
street; it had once been a very large room,
but had been divided, as was evident from
the cornice being abruptly cut off at the partition. The commercial man and Mr. Birdlime
now occupied adjoining rooms. The partition
which separated them was neither brick nor
lath and plaster, but wood pannelling covered
with canvass, and papered. In passing along

the passage you could occasionally obtain glimpses of the interior of Mr. Birdlime's bedroom, strewn all over with letters, papers, posters, wine bottles, and two or three black boxes, and a pistol case. The door of the bedroom was carefully guarded, except when Mr. Birdlime took an airing, when the servant went up to make the bed and put the room in order without touching any papers.

The head of the bed was towards the wooden partition, and on one side of the bed hung a card giving the times and destination of coaches, waggons, and letters. The day before the election the servant went up as usual to make the bed. The commercial traveller knocked at the bedroom door and asked her to run down and fetch him some hot water for shaving, and he went into his bedroom; but as soon as the girl was out of sight he entered Mr. Birdlime's room and thrust a bradawl through the panel of the partition, so that the hole was covered by the card. This was all he wanted. From the inside of his own room, with a sharp penknife, he made a small hole into Mr. Birdlime's bedroom. The hole on the other side was covered with the card, and by moving the card a little on one side with a pen, he could see everything that was going on, and by applying his ear to the hole, like a stethoscope, he could hear a good deal of the conversation. The passing of money was most active on the day of election, when the commercial traveller was rather unwell and kept his room. When he had locked his own door, and heard Mr. Birdlime's open, he commenced his observations, noted them down in a book with the time of the interview. Often not a word was spoken ; the elector handed in a ticket, and Mr. Birdlime gave them money. He saw sums amounting to nearly three hundred paid to the free and independent electors between twelve and four o'clock, and there was reason to believe other sums were paid at other public-houses. The election was lost by a majority of one hundred and forty-three, and these were the neutrals, doubtfuls, and those who had not made up their minds till the day of election. The commercial traveller paid his bill and at once started for London with his samples.

There was great rejoicing at the declaration
of the poll. The Church and Constitution
were once more saved. Next came the rumours
of a petition, and after some months a Parliamentary committee was appointed. Half the
men who sat on the committee owed their
seats to the same corrupt practices. The open
perjury over election petitions might well stir
up the pious anger of men who were anxious
to preserve the sanctity of an oath in the
House of Commons by imprisoning and perse-
cuting men who declined to take it. The
witnesses swore that the money they received
was for work done. Some, that they had
never received any; others, that they didn't
know who gave it; that Mr. Birdlime had
rheumatism so badly that he could not move
his arms, and was too ill to move in bed without assistance; that they had never been
into his bedroom; that no money had been
taken from the bank where the other accounts
were paid. The member knew nothing about
any payment for votes; he had certainly not
given sixpence beyond the accounts before
the committee. If any money, as alleged,

had been paid, he had no idea where it came from; he had subscribed, but not liberally, to charities; a few pounds might have been spent on refreshments for voters who came from a distance, but there was no open-house keeping or drunkenness. The commercial traveller's story was declared to be a pure invention. There was no corroboration. But the landlord threatened a claim for damage to the partition; the hole, half an inch in diameter, was made by a carpenter years ago for ventilation, and it was now closed! This was the kind of thing that went on for three weeks, when the petition was dismissed, with costs, which were nearly double the expense of the contest on both sides.

Election petitions are a scandal and disgrace, and it is far safer and better to put up with a defeat than to prosecute a petition. I hated elections; they engendered bitterness and strife among neighbours and friends, and lowered public morality. The failure of what everybody knew to be a just petition only intensified the ill-feeling, and caused envy and regret among those who might have had a few pounds, but were not corrupt enough to make the bargain. Some of the baser sort who took the money openly, and jeered the others as fools for not taking it. I remained behind to lecture in the neighbouring villages.

In a short time there was another election in a borough which had the reputation of being the most corrupt hole in the country. It was said that there were a number of pot-wollopers and free and independent electors who lived on elections. The League was there, working under great difficulties; neither Mr. Cobden, nor Mr. Bright, nor Colonel Thompson, nor the candidate could obtain a hearing. Every evening the meetings were broken up by the drunken rowdyism of the neighbourhood. The well-disposed were afraid to leave their homes, and the place was given over to a mob of hired ruffians who yelled doggerel songs, " God save the Queen!" and "Protection to native industry!" till they were hoarse. The authorities never interfered, and if any one was summoned for an assault it was dismissed with the wise remark that they did not want the freedom of election interfered with by hired agitators and foreigners from Manchester.

Colonel Gunson was a fighter; the others were crying for peace where there was no peace. The gallant colonel said a dozen men who had been taught the noble art would settle the business in a few minutes, and he privately communicated with a friend in London to send down a few boxing professionals for the nomination day. Wackem, who was an old electioneering hand, came to me and said, "Buckley, you will have to go off by the mail train to-night for Godbury with a few men to keep order on nomination day." He called a cab, and we drove to a public-house in the Haymarket. Wackem asked if he could speak privately to the landlord. They went upstairs together, while I had tea with the barmaid, who asked me if I knew where it was to come off. I could see where I was by the portraits of distinguished men who adorned the walls, all in fighting costume and attitude. We were to call again in about an hour. I went up Regent Street and looked in the shop windows, when the landlord passed with three or four frightful-looking men at his heels. On my return I was shown upstairs, which was a practising-room, with all sorts of gloves and foils, and stuffed men and contrivances for trying your strength. It was also a portrait gallery. In a few minutes Wackem and the landlord came up. I was much attached to Wackem. He was a fine old man, and our friendship continued until he died, at an advanced age, near London during an exciting church-rate contest.

The landlord called up his men; he said we must either have nine, eleven, or thirteen; if we had even numbers he had noticed that something unpleasant was sure to happen. Wackem decided on nine, and they were called up and stood in line. I never saw such a lot. Scarcely any of them had a proper nose; their clothes varied from green velvet waistcoats to tight-fitting corduroy trousers, patent leather boots and white spats. Some had rings and chains large enough to hold a horse. The landlord said : " These gentlemen want you to go to Godbury to keep the peace at an election. You will all come properly dressed for the occasion, and be here not later than half-past seven, when these two gentlemen will take you to the station, and I shall settle with you on your return when I hears from those two gentlemen that your conduct has been satisfactory. You will be under the command of the Little Bantam, who will see you have no drink or use bad language, but conduct yourselves as is professernal gentlemen should do, and if you have to protect your own corpses or any of the gentlemen's, be careful not to hurt anybody ; and remember orange is the colour. Every one with any other colour is your epitome and an henemy, but don't begin till you see a hopening."

The cabs came up a little before eight ; the Bantam put his men into them. The land-lord shook hands with each of them, and hoped they'd come back in a day or two sound in wind and 'arty. There was quite a mob outside the public. Wackem and I entered the first cab, and the others followed. As we drove along heads would appear at the cab window anxiously inquiring the whereabouts. On our arrival at the station a crowd had collected, but they were in a fog as to what was going on. One said a naval engagement at the Nore; another, a game of four corners. One of the officials asked, in a confidential kind of way, what was going on. I said the men were going into the country for a change of air. Wackem had taken the precaution to secure the tickets beforehand. We arrived at a siding between two stations at which no train was usually allowed to stop. It was about ten o'clock. The Bantam called out the professional names of his men and counted them. On our arrival at the first wayside public—for we had nearly six miles to walk—they must have some refreshment. Bantam limited each man to a pint of beer and two pennyworth of bread and cheese. A rumour had been circulated, without any foundation, that two hundred weavers were coming from Lancashire to be present at the nomination. The landlord and landlady looked on these men as the advanced guard. Some of the men came from Lancashire, and they had some difficulty in understanding their dialect.

It was now drawing towards midnight, the

road was very lonely, and in parts dark from the overhanging of trees. I kept as close as possible to the Bantam, for he was the general in command. I endeavoured to interest him in politics and the Corn Laws. I mentioned something about Sir Robert Peel disappointing his party. The Bantam said, "What could you expect? Every professional knew he was backing the wrong man, and he lost a lot of money over the job." I asked him if he had heard of Cobden and Bright. "I should think so," he ejaculated. "A gamer pair never stepped into the ring. I saw them at Marston Green, where they had a set to, and I said to Jimmy Bellon, who was backing Hogbin, 'You have made a mistake, he is too slow a fighter for me'; and so it proved. The other fellow dashed into him right and left, and I could see it was all over after the first four rounds. There was a lot of money lost over it." I asked him if he had heard of Colonel Gunson or Mr. Taylor. He said he knew the former a little; he had once been to a benefit at his house, and he trained Taylor for his fight with Pat Sullivan. The

Bantam, and I believe all the others, were as
ignorant of the agitation that was going on in
the political world as they were of the form of
government in the moon or the Church Catechism. They lived and thought and fought
and died in their own narrow ring. All they
wanted to know was, "What are the
colours?"

We arrived at Godbury between twelve
and one in the morning. Everything was
quiet. Here and there a few drunken men
were asleep, too helpless to rise or complain
if you fell over them. Now the men were
here I did not know what to do with them.
They followed me like dogs to the inn where
the head committee was supposed to be sitting
both day and night. The agent had just gone
to bed, and as I went upstairs the Bantam and
his men followed. They had received instructions not to lose sight of me, and I had some
difficulty in keeping the Bantam out of the
bedroom. I explained to Mr. Hickley, the
agent, who, I believe, feigned ignorance of the
matter, and who asked, "Where are they?" I
said, "Here they are, all waiting in the passage

to know where to go." He rose up in bed and said, "For God's sake take them away. Give me my trousers; find my keys—this is the one, unlock that box, and take nine half-crowns and give one to each to find his own lodgings," which they had no difficulty in doing in the straw-loft. After a little more beer and bread and cheese and a smoke they were ready to ascend the loft, which had been made comfortable. Every man, before he put foot on the ladder, was searched by Bantam to see he had no pipe or matches.

I went to bed, but had no sleep. I was up early and walked round the old place. I went to the stable and saw the men were at their toilet, preparing for breakfast. Large pails, such as are used in stables, were filled with water, and one after another they dipped in their heads. A hard stable brush and comb were used to part their hair back and front, *i.e.*, such of them as had hair long enough to part. When these men were brushed up they were not so bad, and if it had not been for their noses some of them would have been good-looking and taken for the aristocracy.

They had a good breakfast in the stable, and then walked out, not more than two together. About ten they were to take up their position, not exactly in line, but so that the hoarding of the hustings protected their rear. My heart began to sink. I wished myself out of it. The pounding of drums, the blowing of cow-horns, and the yelling of the crowd increased as one after another made his appearance on the hustings. The Farmers' Friend was heard without much opposition, but the Free Traders had to be content with swinging their arms about like the sails of a windmill.

As time went on, and one after another endeavoured with fine words to administer soothing syrup to the bellowing of cattle, a brewer's dray with beer came upon the scene. There is nothing to prevent a charitably dis-posed person giving away any quantity of beer. The judges have settled what appears to ordinary minds a burlesque and a travesty on common sense. The Bantam walked by where I was standing, and said in a low whisper, "You will see some fun presently." I had noticed that nearly all the disturbance

at meetings was originated and continued by
a few coarse, vulgar roughs, and their over-
bearing manners were such as to make ordinary
persons afraid of them. These had congregated
immediately in front of the hustings, and were
particularly disagreeable.

The leader was a tall, full-stomached, foul-
mouthed bully. It was reported that he and
a few others were hired at 7s. 6d. a day. He
kept grinning and pretending to spit in the
face of one of Cobden's weavers. "He could
wipe his nose with a dozen of 'em and eat
'em afore breakfast." He moved his hand
just in front of the face of the smallest of
the weavers, who asked him not to bring it
too near because he didn't like it. He just
touched the front of the little fellow's face
with the palm of his hand, as if he were
smoothing down his beard. In an instant,
like a flash of lightning, thud after thud,
first on the head and then on the body,
and the bully rolled over, covered with blood.
The other men closed up a little, a few more
came to the front ; but they were knocked over
like ninepins. The dexterity and cleverness

of the performance won the admiration of all parties, because it was not a contentious subject; every one who escaped having his head punched was pleased. The men advanced in an irregular line, but in support of each other. In ten minutes there were twenty or thirty of the ringleaders and roughs with bloody noses and swollen eyes, and others were white with fear. Some said if this performance had taken place earlier in the contest we should have won the election.

I became so excited that I felt a strong desire to go and strike somebody, and was rather disappointed that no safe opportunity offered. Suddenly a farm labourer, who was getting the worst of it in front, stepped back on to my toes, and this gave me the desired opportunity. I struck him on the back of his head, which was like a stone, and hurt myself much more than I hurt him. I noticed that the disturbance at meetings generally originated with a few persons — sometimes hired for the purpose—and if these could be put down or put out, everything went on quietly. There are times when the exercise of great physical power is necessary, it strikes men with awe, and secures the applause and admiration of enemies.

There was, of course, great howling and wailing in all the Protectionist papers about hired ruffians and prizefighters attacking harmless, inoffensive persons, who had been prompted by a natural anxiety to hear the candidates. Any one who has had experience must know that the rowdyism generally begins with the supporters of the constitution. The clergy and the constables were the persons who generally threatened me, and ordered my removal from the village green. There was no more disturbance of any importance. We lost the election, but we won the battle, and in the middle of the night the men returned in twos and threes to the nearest station. I reported to Wackem—on the authority of Bantam—that no one was killed or hurt, and the conduct of the men was in all respects satisfactory.

The following day I went to London. Wackem took me to a little public-house up a court. The floor was covered with sawdust,

at one end was the portrait of a man drawing
a cork, and the seats were old wooden settles.
It was a curious old place. Wackem ordered
two chops and two toasted cheeses, a pint of
stout, and a bottle of ginger beer. It was the
most enjoyable dinner I ever had. I related
to Wackem all that had taken place, and he
was immensely delighted, and thought it was
the right thing to do. We took a cab to the
Haymarket. The landlord and Wackem went
upstairs, and I again had tea with the barmaid—she was rather a good-looking barmaid. We took another cab and spoke at a
meeting at Clerkenwell in the evening, but
I asked Wackem, as a particular favour, to
ask our Council have me sent into the country.

To begin speechifying at nine or ten o'clock
at night in some stuffy club-room reeking
with tobacco and the fumes of liquor was not
to my taste, but no other place, except for
members of Parliament, could be obtained.
Schools were as difficult to obtain as churches.
At a public-house you met the tradespeople
of the neighbourhood after they had closed
their shops, and I don't suppose they would

have gone to any other place. When not otherwise engaged I used to go to a public-house in Bride Lane, to which I had been introduced by Wackem. The Cogers' Hall was a memorable place for the discussion of current politics. There was a chairman, who acted as Speaker, and everything was conducted in strict parliamentary style. The room would accommodate about forty or fifty persons, and these were of a miscellaneous order—decayed agitators, journalists, reporters, lawyers, barristers, doctors, editors, and lecturers. Some, I believe, had been members of Parliament, and there were a few who hoped to be. The oratory was often of a very effective kind, and quite equal to the usual oratory in the House of Commons. I often asked myself, What was the use of this talent? Some few, I believe, did rise, but I fear the majority disappeared. One afternoon Wackem took me to see one of the Cogers, who lodged in a small room off Chancery Lane. He was wanted for a large meeting at Kennington, for which he would be paid a guinea. The room was foul and wretched in the extreme. On a piece of dirty bedding in the corner, partly undressed, the man who could hold an audience equal to O'Connell was lying stricken down and helpless as a child. Wackem, who, I believe, loved him, shed tears, and had him removed to another lodging, sent for a doctor, and had him comfortably provided for. In a few days Wackem and three or four Cogers stood around his grave and wept. And so passed away, like a shooting-star, a handsome young man of twenty-five, who had only one fault. It seemed to me that there was no unmixed good in this world; the excitement of debate was often fed by other excitements, and after one night at the Cogers' it took three days on a common to purify your clothes. But there was no place in London where you could gain so much knowledge in a short time on current social and political questions.

CHAPTER XI.

I AGAIN begged of Wackem to send me
to the country—he was in a sense my
superior—but he preferred my going about
with him. At last he consented. I had only
been away three days when I was recalled.
There was to be a City election, and it was
to be fought in the Free Trade interest. A
few days elapsed before a suitable candidate
could be obtained. The Tory had already
issued his address about protection to native
industries and the un-English proposal for

secret voting. Then followed the address of the Free Trade candidate ; and the result of the contest was looked forward to with almost national interest. As time went on the excitement increased. I had charge of one of the most respectable and Conservative districts south of Kennington Church. I took up my headquarters at a large public-house in the main road. The landlord was a decent man and a thorough Free Trader. After placarding the windows from top to bottom—that the committee sat daily and, I ought to have added, nightly—I saw that the front of the house was properly decorated with pictorial and other Free Trade literature.

The leisure of the first two or three days I devoted to the study of a map and directory of the district and the poll books. I knew if I depended on paid canvassers I should only be deceived, so I determined to do as much of the canvassing as possible. Though I endeavoured to be polite and civil I often met with annoyance and sometimes insult from flunkies and persons who lived in large houses on the common ; here and there, like an oasis

in the desert, I met with a Free Trader, and
from him I obtained reliable information. In
calling over the names he would say, "dead
against us," "favourable," "don't know,"
"you might call." I said I should call on
every voter, and, if possible, see him, but not
to argue with him; it is a waste of time to
argue on a canvass. Some went to London
very early and could only be seen before eight;
others only came home just in time for dinner.
To see a hungry voter before his dinner, if
favourable, was very imprudent—it might
make him vote the other way—and if opposed
dangerous. I used to loiter about the common
till after dinner; I could often see how they
were getting on from the outside, and on one
occasion when I was watching through the
railings to see when the ladies retired, a
policeman came up and asked my business.
He knew an election was coming on, and
under a gas-lamp I showed him my papers
and then asked him if he had a vote for the
City, and he laughed and said, "You are
poking fun at me"; and as he was very civil
I tipped him and he gave me much helpful

information about the domestic habits of men
I wanted to see. I had often to wait an hour
in the morning before the front door opened
and the gentleman walked out, to whom I had
been previously denied by the flunkey. I now
assumed, as far as possible, a pleasant expression of countenance and the most polite
behaviour: " I beg your pardon, sir, I believe
I have the honour of addressing. Mr. Crook-
nose?" "Yes; what do you want?" "I
beg most respectfully to solicit your vote
and interest on behalf of Mr. Matterson."
"Nothing of the kind; his opinions are most
dangerous and destructive. I am on Mr.
Flaring's committee, and he will be returned
by a large majority, so you need not trouble
yourself." "Thank you; good morning!"
I canvassed one gentleman after dinner and
he said, "If you don't take yourself off, I'll
kick you out." What he would have done if
I had called before dinner is too terrible to
contemplate.

In this way I saw a large number of voters,
mostly disagreeable. A few days before the
election I made my return to the office, which

was not so encouraging as I expected. I made
a list with the addresses of all who wished to
be taken to the poll and the time most convenient, and arranged their conveyances.
After nearly three weeks' worry and work,
the election was announced for Saturday, and
before ten o'clock on that day I discharged
six cabmen for being drunk. I rose early on
the polling day and visited the extreme end
of the division before some of the voters were
out of bed ; I knew it was important to make
a good start. We were in a majority after the
first hour and kept it till the close of the poll,
which ended at four with a majority of upwards of two hundred.

The City had, for the first time, pronounced
in favour of Free Trade. The result was
attributed, as is usual with the defeated party,
to every cause but the right one, namely, the
want of votes. I saw the result duly posted
outside the public-houses for the information
of persons going to church on Sunday. It
was getting dark, and a crowd of persons had
assembled outside. Some were rather noisy
and boisterous; I begged of them to go quietly

home, a scuffle ensued, and some one hit me in the eye. The wife of the landlord bathed my eye and tied on a piece of raw beef, and I took the Sussex coach, which was passing, and in a short time I was in the office in London. Here there was great rejoicing, and when I made my appearance, Mr. Paulton, Mr. Cobden, and men whom I had never seen laugh, gave way to great hilarity. From before six till nearly ten I had been hard at work. I was bonneted, I had fallen in the road, my clothes were dirt-stained and torn, I had had nothing but a penny roll and a bottle of ginger-beer during the day; but we had returned our candidate, which atoned for everything. I went upstairs to make myself presentable. I had a cup of tea and some bread-and-butter, and lay down on a sofa till I was awakened at eleven o'clock the next morning by the church bells. The son of the new member came and breakfasted with me and thanked me for what I had done, and we drove in a cab to a friend's house a few miles off, where I remained till my eye was nearly well. The member's son was very agreeable, but much more of a sportsman than a politician.

On my return to London I went to Tooting, Enfield, Croydon, and other places with Wackem, and occasionally to the Cogers' Hall. But what I had seen since my last visit awakened painful memories and I never cared about the place afterwards. I was careful to keep as much as possible east of Charing Cross, because I was frequently met by some of the weaver boys, who were no respecter of persons ; for they used to come up and shake hands in the most friendly way, and this was not always agreeable when alone, and highly unpleasant when in company with others to whom I could not explain the reason of their familiarity.

There was now a rumour of a contest in the North, and, with two or three others, we started for the West Riding. We held several successful meetings. A nobleman who was present at one of them, and who was to be the candidate in the event of a contest, asked me to call on him when he came to London. I mentioned the invitation to one of my friends and said I did not think I should call. He said, "Don't you be a fool." I began to be tired of this kind of life, and I mentioned the matter to Mr. Bright, but he thought I might go on a little longer. I saw that the Corn Laws must be repealed, and there was nothing I was fit for but to return to my trade. But the last two or three years had unfitted me for that. Mr. Cobden suggested my taking up the Education Question; Mr. Taylor, Church Rates; Mr. Sturge, the Ballot and the Franchise. There were already influential organisations for promoting these objects. I felt utterly unfitted for educational work by reason of my own defective education, and the other subjects had never inspired me, and so I kept on with my first attachment.

I was in the office one afternoon when the city member's son came in. He appeared pleased to meet me, said his father was always glad to hear of me. He said: " You will meet me at three next Saturday week at the ' White Horse,' and I will drive you down to Ascot." There was not much doing at the time, and at three o'clock I was at the " White Horse," Piccadilly. We had a nice trap and a spirited horse. At Ascot we put up

at a large white house on the side of the road
looking over the heath and racecourse. The
stables were fast filling with horses, trainers,
jockeys, grooms, and hangers-on. Every hour
brought fresh arrivals, and on Sunday fifteen
sat down to dinner, and this number continued
till the following Friday. A French cook and
his assistants prepared dishes, the like of
which I had never tasted; but I had no
pleasure from this kind of thing. I was
out of place. Nothing was talked about but
backing horses. One day I saw a little fellow
all covered up, except his head, in a dung-
heap, and I was informed he was reducing
his weight! In the evening, after the races,
there were several pre-arranged fights on the
heath, and after dinner we used to sit out of
doors till one or two o'clock in the morning.
Two of the company were, or had been,
celebrated opera singers, who now owned
racehorses, and had sung with Madame
Vestris, and in the quiet of the evening, about
eleven or twelve o'clock, their voices could be
heard at the training-stables, more than
half a mile distant. The country for miles

was nothing but heath, with a few houses, and these a long distance from each other. It was a desolate place at night even in summer. Near the house, with the sanction of the owners, was a gipsy encampment.

Between the gipsies and the house party there was great freedom. In the morning they provided games, knockemdowns, and in the evening music and dancing. Two old barn doors were laid on the grass, and the father of the family sat on a chair and played the fiddle. The gipsy girls were very good dancers; some of them had attractive faces and good figures. They were dressed in red, black, and yellow silk, with black hair and eyes, and olive skin. It was difficult to resist having your fortune told. They swarmed round the carriages during the interval of races, and must have taken each day a large sum of money. There was nothing rude, coarse, or vulgar in their behaviour. Some of the ladies in carriages were more vulgar. With the residents the gipsies conducted themselves with the greatest propriety; they never intruded or asked to tell your fortune.

I was told they were of a superior family, and had been on the heath for years. One gentleman gave one of the gipsies a ten-pound note to change, and he could, no doubt, have changed it himself; but he preferred changing it at Sunningdale, and as no one there would change it he went on to Egham; and, as he did not return quite so soon as was expected, some one remarked, " Your ten pounds has gone all right." But, after two or three hours, the gipsy, covered with dust and perspiration, returned with the ten sovereigns. I preferred sitting and talking with these gipsies to the racing gentlemen, and I began to think they had been much misrepresented. I was heartily glad when the week came to an end; it would have been intolerable but for the society of the gipsies. I was rather more attached to one of them because it was her mother who had nursed me when sick with small-pox. We often think we know a good deal of the character of a class from what tradition and our prejudices teach us.

We returned to London in small parties. The change and fresh air did me good, but I never had any desire for the society of a race-course. I thanked the gentlemen and said I enjoyed myself as much as my ignorance of the parentage and names of the horses would permit. I now went into the country occasionally, holding meetings and visiting old friends, who were pleased to see me.

CHAPTER XII

A West Riding M.P. sends me to the training college—
A place of cabbage gardens—A new teacher, a Jew
—Work with the hands—Church history and my
heresy—"Gil Blas"—Science lecturing—Assist Poor
Law inspector—Horrors and incidents of an infant
asylum—Return to the Institution in a sad frame of
mind.

ON my return to London I called on the
member for the West Riding. He said
he had made some inquiries, and he thought
it was a pity to give up my future to the
agitation of political questions. The Corn
Laws would certainly be repealed, and there
was no chance of their re-imposition. He
thought I had abilities which might be turned
to better use, and as the Education Question
must be taken up by the Government, he
suggested that two or three years at a train-

ing school would be of great service, and open up a useful career. He had given a large subscription to an Institution for the training and education of teachers, and he would further defray all other expenses. I had saved a little money, but a man's capital soon dissolves when he begins to live on it, and I had somewhat reduced it by visiting and making presents. His lordship wished me to seriously think the matter over and let him know my decision. I had no materials for thinking, and I felt I had now come to the parting of the roads, uncertain which to take. I called on his lordship, and he gave me a letter to Dr. Kaye, who sent me to a training school. On my way I almost resolved to turn back; but I felt I should be acting badly to my friends, and perhaps lose their patronage and good opinion. I passed through endless cabbage gardens to what was called a square, a triangular piece of ground surrounded by quaint old houses and shops. And a few yards from the extreme point, facing the Thames, was a large square house, standing in about two acres of ground; it had a large garden, with several large cedar and other trees, and had once been the residence of a wealthy City merchant. It was now called a college. It was pleasantly situated, and inside there was evidence of comfort and substantial workmanship.

On my arrival I was received by the head of the Institution with every expression of goodfellowship. A number of curious-looking young men stood staring at me as if I were a new curiosity. One of them, who afterwards became a parson, was called to show me over the buildings and then bring me back to the principal. I saw the printer's shop, the carpenter's shop, the smith's shop, the class-rooms, the dining-hall, the library, the cubicles, or sleeping berths, and the lecture-rooms. I was then taken to the practising school, where men were giving object-lessons. The garden was cultivated by the students, under the superintendence of a manciple. Three times a week a drill serjeant came from the military hospital. I happened to be present just as the students, about forty in number, were ordered to fall in, and I never saw such a miscellaneous collection ; some men were over six feet, others were dwarfs ; some grey-haired, and others lads about sixteen ; and all rather poorly dressed in seedy black and white chokers. None of them, fortunately, had any idea of my former life, but in the course of conversation I found out that they were a mixture of all sorts : clever lads from pauper schools, under-butlers to deans and bishops, footmen, Sunday-school teachers, drapers' assistants, tailors, clerks, and a few mechanics. The idea of two or three years with these men, when I had done nothing to deserve it, only added to my doubt and uncertainty as to the future.

I cannot enter into all the details of my life and trials at this Institution, though my experiences were often peculiar and painful. Eventually the college was put under a Church principal, and new troubles began. I made progress, and constructed models, but when one of the examinations arrived an incident occurred that may be worth relating. The Principal was intent on Church doctrine and history, of which I knew little.

All the books in his library on the subject were taken away a few days before the examination. Fortunately, as I thought, I had picked up a ninepenny history of the Church at a bookstall likely to be of service to me. When the list came out after the second examination I found my name was omitted. This was a surprise.

The principal sent for me, and asked what I meant by saying that the character of Cranmer was unworthy of admiration; he ought not to have been burned, but ought to have been imprisoned; that Parker was consecrated after dinner at a public-house in Cheapside by a person who had no authority to consecrate him, which threw doubts on apostolical succession. These — and some other observations about Wickliffe being disappointed of a Fellowship was too much for an Anglican Principal. Where had I obtained these ideas? I told him that I got them from a Church History, which he desired me to produce. I fetched the book, and as soon as he had looked at it he threw it on the fire. He asked me if any one else in the place had seen it. I replied, " No." He said it was a tissue of Popish lies, and he was hurt beyond measure that such poison had been introduced into the place. I replied that it seemed a much easier Church History than those in the library, and that was why I purchased it. How there could be two histories of a Church was beyond my understanding. I pleaded pure ignorance as my excuse for giving pain to one whom I would not knowingly hurt or offend.

The dinner-bell rang, and as I left he said, " I won't trouble you to attend my Church History lectures again."

Another incident occurred which may also be referred to, because it also concerned a book. The Principal, after lecturing me on the sin of idleness when I had resolved to remain at the Institution and study, during the conversation gave me a book to study. I went on the adjoining common to read it. To my astonishment it began : " De la naissance de Gil Blas et de son education." " Blas de santillane mon père après avoir longtemps porte les armes pour le service de la monarchie Espagnole se retua vetua dans la ville ou il avait pris naissance." What was I to do? I could never be expected to read a book in a language of which I was utterly ignorant, and to read it with the aid of a dictionary involved an amount of work and time which I could ill afford. I did, however, manage after a fashion to translate one or two sentences. Was this book given to me as a joke, or by mistake for some theological work?

I devoted my vacation to science, and the making of models, which were approved. After one of my lessons I was asked to give lectures outside the college, and obtained the permission of the principal to do so. The Government inspector, who resided not far off, made arrangements for me to attend his house twice a week and give lessons to his two boys with half a dozen others. I taught this class for twelve months, when a piece of Church patronage removed him. More than thirty years after I met one of his sons at the Society of Arts. He was then Linacre professor at Oxford. When my name was mentioned he looked at me. I hesitated as to who ought to speak first, as our positions in life were now very different; but I resolved on making myself known. He took me warmly by the hand, and said, "I should never have been where I am but for your teaching, which gave me a love for science I have ever since cultivated. The other day I was one of the examiners for the Radcliffe, and there was a candidate of your name up that brought you forcibly home to my memory. I sent for him, but he had gone down. I have since learned he was your son, and I congratulate you on his success. You must promise to come to Oxford and spend a week with me, when we can talk over the past with a cigar in the garden."

I had just settled down to work when I was informed that my services were required for a week or two to assist the Poor Law inspector in the examination of a large pauper school a few miles from town.

My first impression was that institutions of this kind should be under a special department of the Government, and not left to guardians and contractors in flesh and blood. I took

an early opportunity of visiting the place and
seeing what sort of children had to be examined, and as I should be engaged for three
or four weeks, I thought the first thing was
to secure decent lodgings. A little distance
from the asylum was a quaint, old-fashioned
country inn, very attractive outside, and, as
far as I could judge, clean and comfortable
inside. It was kept by a widow and her two
daughters, who at first were most attentive,
but in a few days avoided me. If we met on
the staircase they ran back. I said, "I am
afraid you will find me a poor lodger, as I
never drink intoxicating drinks, but in consideration of this I will pay a trifle more for
my lodgings." I now called on the head of
the infant pauper asylum. He appeared to
me as a very fine portly English farmer,
about fifty years of age. He received me
with generous hospitality ; he sorrowed over
the loss of his wife, whom he described as
his right hand. She looked after the girls
better than the nurses, some of whom were
not infected with any love for total abstinence. I looked over the visitors' book, and

found the names of bishops, lords, baronets, members of Parliament, clergy, and the guardians from twelve unions who at different times had visited the establishment and expressed in terms of the highest approval their admiration for everything they saw. But the truth is often to be found in what we don't see. The master wanted me to sign my name in the visitors' book, but I declined (a rather ungracious thing to do after a good luncheon) until I had seen over the place. He sent for a man to show me over. I politely but firmly declined his services, because I knew what showing you over a public institution meant. I said, " You must allow me to go about by myself." The first thing I saw was an open stinking sewer ditch into which the filth and sewage of 1,400 persons filtered, and this ran parallel with the dormitories and schools. I saw the bedrooms were without fireplaces, and that windows could not be opened, that floors were rotten with constant washing, and the quantity of air was quite inadequate to the wants of the children. The dietary was chiefly

of bread, pea soups, potatoes, and suet-
puddings—not a very complete dietary for
growing children. Although it was the middle
of winter not one of the children wore flannel,
and they went about in cotton pinafores
shivering with cold. With all this their faces
looked fairly plump, but their arms and legs
were like drumsticks, and their bodies ema-
ciated. There was one nurse to twenty-five or
thirty children ; they were of the old style and
aged. They each had a bottle of medicine
for the children, and most of them had a
bottle of something else for themselves.
Nearly everything was contract — children
clothed, fed, and educated at 4s. 6d. a week ;
medicine and attendance on 1,400 children for
£70 a-year. I had really nothing to do with
these matters, but as it was reported to the
world in all the papers as a wonderful and successful experiment by which the infant pauper
problem was solved, I was curious to know
everything. My business was to find out if
these children, whose ages varied from one
to fourteen, were being properly educated and
instructed in the principles of the Church of

England. I now looked through the schools—
indeed, I was to visit officially the following
week—and here the odour was sickening, but
those inside appeared quite unconscious of
anything unpleasant, and were rather surprised at my observation about the air. They
had no windows open, because they were not
intended to open and expose the children to
draughts. I saw a number of them had sore
eyes, others had boils and open sores on the
neck ; but, taken in the mass, there was
nothing to impress you with the idea that
the children were not cared for, but when
naked they all had enlarged stomachs. I saw
two girls vomiting, and when I called the
attention of the teacher to it, she replied
they had eaten something which disagreed
with them. The buildings were old, the
chief one was comfortable and substantial,
but this was occupied by the master of the
establishment and the head officials. The
remainder of the buildings were the outbuildings of an old manor-house, but the
others were temporary wooden barracks,
easily extended with every new importa-

tion of children. The girls appeared heavy, sullen, and helpless, frightened if you spoke to them ever so kindly; they seemed destitute of all love or affection; they had no dolls to nurse, which is so natural to young girls. The boys worked on the land, about forty acres, but were not properly taught any trade, and I was told that many of the elder boys had low, debased habits, and used foul and obscene language to the girls.

I returned to my lodgings and began to think I had undertaken a rather unpleasant business. When at breakfast on the Monday I was to begin work, the news came that there was a sudden outbreak of cholera among the children, and twenty-five had died within an hour. The medical officer from the Board of Health called, and assured me I need not alarm myself, as the outbreak was no more contagious than chilblains. I accompanied him to the asylum, and I shall never forget the scene—women crying and shrieking for their children, some of them drunk; a mixed mob outside and inside, running about without knowing what to do or where to go. Medical men and guardians from the different unions arrived in batches, until the place looked like the opening of a medical congress. Some of the children cried piteously for water, but there was none fit to drink. They then passed into a deep sleep, from which they never awoke. Some fell down and died in the yard, others were removed to beds saturated with the vomits or excretions of previous occupants, and for several days and nights the scene was sorrowful beyond description. In four days 150 died and were buried in less than twenty-four hours after death in boxes, each box holding from four to six bodies, without any identification or inquest. The unions were ordered to immediately remove their children, but many of them had no place to remove them to; numbers were taken to infirmaries and hospitals, where the total deaths reached 352. Covered vans and omnibuses passed through the streets at night laden with the waste refuse of our humanity.

There was a strong public feeling that cholera would be spread through London by their removal, but no case occurred except among these children. A coroner's inquest brought in a verdict of manslaughter against this contractor in the flesh and blood of poor children. He was acquitted, of course, but he died soon after; the strain was too much for him. When I first saw him, a few months before, he was a hale, hearty man, with dark hair and florid complexion; he now stood in the dock a wreck of his former self, with hair and beard as white as snow. What had brought about this change? The four-and-sixpenny greed, the desire to make money out of the flesh and blood of poor children, who were underfed, insufficiently clothed during a severe winter in fustian and calico, because it was cheaper than flannel; condemned to breathe an atmosphere saturated with poisonous germs, which their imperfectly nourished bodies were unable to resist, when death in its most repulsive form came early to their relief. I remained about three weeks, until only thirteen children were left, whom no one owned. When the children had left a detachment of navvies arrived to clear out the ditches and open sewers when there was no one to die.

I had no opportunity of judging the educational attainments of these children; I have no doubt they corresponded with their physical condition. The teachers were a poor lot, but quite equal to their salaries. If they had failed in everything else they would probably have passed excellently well in the Catechism.

I was sitting in the office one evening, trying to solve the puzzles and contradictory orders almost daily issued by the Board of Health to the guardians, when I was told two ladies wished to see me. The place, once all life and excitement, now began to assume the gloomy dulness of the grave. The two ladies—for they were becomingly dressed as ladies — had come to inquire about their children. I could not understand how women apparently in their positions could have children at a pauper asylum. None of the children left belonged to them, and I could find no trace of them; they were probably resting, with others, in the churchyard. The women were very sorrowful; they shed tears, which appeared to involuntarily run down their cheeks without stint. Sorrow is contagious; I have seen and experienced a good deal of it, but I never remember being so touched with the sorrows of others. I tried to comfort them with the usual platitudes about their children having escaped the trials and sorrows of this life, which, under its most favourable conditions, was not always a blessing to be desired, but remarks of this kind afford no comfort to the heart of a loving woman sorrowing for her children; when the shadow of those we love has passed away the vision still haunts us. I invited them to have tea, but they at first refused, but after another invitation consented. In a short time we grew more friendly and confidential. I assured them that what they said would be strictly private between us, and I was in full sympathy with the sorrow which had overtaken them. The elder of these ladies was, and had been for years, house-keeper to a Cabinet Minister. She had been unfortunate a few years before with one of the men-servants, who promised her marriage and then deserted her. She had to practice all sorts of deceit to hide her misfortune and keep her situation, and this she succeeded in doing through the help of a married sister, who took the child when it was three weeks old. In a few months it was admitted to the pauper asylum in the name of the married sister, who was regarded as the official mother of the child. She made all the payments, and occasionally visited the child; the child was to have a bed to itself and have other little attentions as regards food for extra payment of one shilling a week, which I fear it never had. Thirty years after, by the accident of losing my train, I met this woman again; she had married a well-to-do farmer on the estate, and appeared very happy. She had forgotten my name, but when her husband went out to chain up the dog she said, "You will not forget the promise you made me many years ago." I replied, "It is sacred as the confessional"; but as she had no children, and all the parties are now dead, there is no harm in referring to it.

The other case was in some respects more sad. This young woman was a lady's-maid, and had been led away by the son of her

mistress, who promised to marry her, but after
her trouble cared nothing about her, and the
family refused to see her or have anything to
do with her. But the wretch who had brought
this sorrowful ruin on the woman could sit at
the same table every day with elegantly
dressed ladies and drink champagne and talk
about the vice and profligacy of the poor.
The mother, who took charge of the child,
eventually passed it into the pauper asylum
in a feigned name, and so long as the child
lived it was visited once a week and cared for
as well as it could be in such a place. A
period of much secret sorrow and trouble
followed. She was advised a lawsuit, but her
lawyer told her the corroborative evidence was
not sufficient, and failure would only deepen
her sorrow. The lady could not think of
giving a low, common, deceitful woman a character, and but for the kindness of her mother,
who was able to help her, there was nothing
for this poor creature but the street. There
is no organised trades union among lady's-
maids, but they know each other, and where
friendships spring up are ready to help each

other.   After a time, through the influence of a lady's-maid who knew all the trouble she had passed through, this young woman became lady's-maid to the daughters of a baronet, where she remained for years.

Two or three women would sometimes come drunk and inquire for their dear little bastards; these were shown the door. But who knew their history or cared to know it? The sorrow, the degradation belong to the woman; she loses caste among her friends and neighbours, but the man, who ought to be avoided as a social leper unless he marries the woman he has wronged, loses nothing. He is admitted into what is called Society, and his mother and sisters speak of it as an unfortunate liaison. The condemnation falls on the woman, as if she alone were the guilty party. It may be very well for old women who never felt the passion of love, who were never young, to lift up their pious hands and condemn the feebleness which yields to the most powerful temptations of human nature, and which, at times, some appear helpless to resist. We know nothing of the circumstances or surroundings which helped to the downfall of these women, who ought rather to be objects of sorrow before we pass sentence on their sin. Nature does not compel persons to marry, but she does influence them by feelings and desires which they are not always able to resist. The sin is not against nature, but against society, which is wantonly cruel to the woman. More than two hundred and thirty children in the asylum were by our laws illegitimate, bearing the name of the mother. How could these children help their birth. Yet through life they must carry with them the mark of Cain!

I returned to the Institution and resumed my work, but the thought of this infant pauper asylum haunted me by day and night. When I called to mind these poor children and saw the brutal cruelty, sanctioned by law, which one man could inflict on defenceless children who came into this world from no will of their own, but because they were fatherless and motherless had greater claims on humanity and entitled to more kindly consideration, cast on the world, drifted about to perish like autumn leaves, I began to doubt—

and at that time it was my first serious doubt —if the laws of man were not at variance with the laws of God, and whether there was any operative force in this world superior to the cruelty of man, or why should this sorrow and suffering exist?

CHAPTER XIII.

Offered appointment at a juvenile convict establishment
—Chaplain's prayer-meetings—Military discipline of
the prison—Two boys flogged—The dietary—My
suggestions scouted—Shipping batches of convicts
for the Colonies—Hepworth Dixon and Charles
Dickens visit the establishment—I show them over,
dine with them, and write articles on the prison—
Carpeted for the articles, and resign—My complaints
justified—Return to the training college—Become
science teacher—The Prime Minister's school—My
visit to him—Dies before a reform scheme could be
put into practice—I get married—Changes in the
college—Attacks on old teachers—A sly man and
his tricks—I leave the college.

O N my return to the training Institution I took
up the science teaching and occasionally
taught for Mr. Meyer. One day the Principal
sent for me and said I had been recommended
to the Home Secretary for an appointment at
a juvenile convict prison, to take charge,

under the chaplain, of the education of the junior division. He thought the situation would suit me, and it was a safe Government appointment, but as the teachers under me were older I must be careful. I consulted the vice-principal and the mathematical master, and they advised me to accept the appointment, and in a week I found myself in the company of about six hundred and fifty convicts, whose ages varied from nine to seventeen years. So barbarous was our criminal code that boys were transported for offences for which they are now birched or sent to an industrial school or dealt with under the First Offenders Act. The judges in passing sentence would frequently remark that it was the only thing they could do. These boys practically began life as convicts; they were often without parents or were the children of convicts, which I thought very terrible. I could not conceive a boy ten or twelve years of age doing anything which justified transportation for life.

On my arrival I was handed over by the porter of the prison to an assistant warder, who handed me to a head warder, who handed

me to the deputy-governor, who introduced
me to the governor and chaplain. I had very
comfortable rooms, and the chaplain invited
me to tea. He had a good house and a large
garden well cultivated by convict labour—the
best of all labour. He hoped we should work
comfortably together. His conversation was
not on educational matters, but saving the souls
of these boys, some of whom I soon found out
had no souls worth saving. He had a special
weekly prayer-meeting at his house, to which
all the officers not on duty were invited, and
he hoped I should join them. I did not despise
them, but they were not in my way, and yet,
as I wished to avoid all appearance of indiffe-
rence to the means of grace which were somehow to find their way to the hearts of those
boys, who were locked up in cells on bread
and water, I went to one prayer-meeting.
First the chaplain made a prayer, followed
by lemonade and biscuits, a verse of a hymn,
then another prayer by a warder. I passed
a more uncomfortable hour than I had done
on the boat. I soon found the praying was
not so much for the boys as for me. For

some reason or other they prayed at me and for me. Only those who have suffered this praying at you can understand it, because you cannot make a prayer in reply. When I left the Institution the Principal wished me to write to him, and if I were in any doubt or trouble to make a friend of him. We shook hands with moist eyes. I wrote him an account of the prayer-meeting, and said I did not think I should go again, and I was afraid the place would not suit me. He replied in a kind letter urging me not to form a hasty opinion, but to submit to the chaplain's authority.

After a few months I began to see the place as it was, not as it appeared under the polished boots and buttons and the militarism which went through the life of the prison. The governor had been a soldier, the deputy-governor had been a soldier, all the warders, assistant warders, and porters had been soldiers, and smartness at drill was their only idea of government and reformation. Talking in the ranks, dirty boots, and laughing, although there was not much to laugh at, were reported and punished with confinement and bread and water. The prison was divided into A ward, B ward, C ward, and so on, and each prisoner was known by a number, which was in brass figures on a black leather cap, which was polished like his boots. The dress was a coarse grey woollen with red or yellow trimmings, stamped all over with prison letters. On the arrival of a prisoner he was weighed, his religion and other particulars entered in a book ; he was then placed in the probationary ward in solitary confinement for three months, except when he was at school. All the prisoners were kept in separate cells, about 8 ft. by 5 ft. ; the bed, of cocoanut matting, was hung from straps at either end of the cell, forming a kind of hammock, which was taken down in the morning, neatly packed up, and placed on a shelf. The dietary consisted of porridge, milk, cocoa, bread, soup, and twice or three times a week meat and potatoes, except those under punishment, who had nothing but bread and water, with so many pounds of oakum to pick. The food was good enough, but scarcely sufficient for growing lads, who needed more food than adults.

Two boys out of B ward had tried to escape and had to be punished. The boys in B ward were marched out to witness the punishment as an example. An iron bedstead was placed against the wall at a suitable angle, the two lads were marched in, dressed in the punishment colour—yellow. One boy was first stripped and strapped to the bedstead, and flogged like a common soldier till the blood ran down his legs, and then sent to the infirmary for a day or two; then the other boy was brought in and flogged. There were present the governor, the doctor, the chaplain, the deputy-governor, the head warders, and some others. I had no business there, because it was a discipline matter which was not supposed to concern me, but I saw it from the gallery of B ward. I had free access to every prisoner and every part of the prison, and a few days after I called on the boys flogged. They were not nearly so bad as some boys who had never attempted their liberty. They were reasonable in their conversation, and contended in justification that there was no crime in trying to gain your liberty. I explained to them that to gain their liberty on an island was impossible. They said, "We did not know it was an island." I asked them if they had a father or mother or sister, and then came the same horrible tale of drink with the younger boys.

I was anxious to introduce the Pestalozzian or Fröbellian system of teaching, which seemed to me the only natural and common-sense system. This was objected to. I then suggested that the school should precede work on the land, or in the shops, or in cleaning. This was objected to as interfering with prayers. I proposed that boys who had shown themselves worthy should have a little more liberty, should not always be attended on little errands by an assistant warder, but trusted. This was objected to. The discipline department was too strong; the desire to make these lads better was a thing they never thought about. Chaplains and schoolmasters were a nuisance. Punishment was the only remedy. I had a notion that the more you punished the less chance you had of any improvement. These boys were not all wild beasts; some of

them were good and much better than many
who had their liberty. The boy who held his
mother's head while his father murdered her
was a different wretch to the boy who committed a petty larceny or a bungling forgery,
not knowing the enormity of his crime, but
they were both convicts and treated alike. I
wanted the boys grouped into families under
good agricultural labourers and their wives,
rather than soldiers, so that they should have
some idea of a home, which many of them
had never seen. But this was laughed at by
the discipline department. I drew up a
report and suggested that the wearisomeness
of convict life might be relieved by short,
simple lectures, for boys of good report, on
subjects of general interest, illustrated by
experiments, and I offered to do this for
nothing. I was anxious to throw some ray of
light where all was dark and repressive. I
was told by the chaplain that people would
get their boys transported for the purpose of
learning science. The object of all my teaching should be directed to a change of heart.
I saw that as long as the discipline depart-

ment was the predominant partner there was no hope, and all fine writing in the reports about the reformatory influences at work in the prison were a cheat; the prisoners never had a chance of showing they were reformed, because they were never trusted to carry an empty ink bottle without a warder.

Every now and then an order would come from the Home Office for one or two hundred to go on board a convict-ship lying in the Solent, on its way to Port Philip or some other station. The boys who had perhaps only one or two years to serve, no matter what their conduct had been, would be selected. No convict was allowed to complete his term of transportation in this country. If they had any relations or friends they were written to, and it then came out that numbers were transported in assumed names. Many of them did not know they had any father or mother or relations. The last interview between mothers and their boys was a scene often too much for the icy hearts of the discipline department. These poor women had often walked a hundred miles or more and sacrificed everything to the pawnshop to see their sons for the last time. The boys were for the most part joyous at the prospect of a long journey and a new country, which they called the land of promise, where they had a chance of becoming magistrates, landowners, and bankers.

The ship, a sailing-vessel, had arrived, and was now waiting to complete its living cargo. There were already a good number of convicts on board. The number was completed by an addition of nearly two hundred. Of all the dreadful products of an old civilisation a convict-ship is the most horrible. A detachment of marines was on deck; below, caged down with heavy irons like wild beasts, you could see between the iron bars every grade of human wretchedness and despair. The captain and officers of the ship seemed to think no more of this human cargo than if it had been made up of bales of cotton. After I landed I almost wished I had been spared the ghastly sight; it haunted me for days. These were my fellow-creatures, some of them perhaps having loving mothers and sisters, others neglected and uncared for from birth, cast

on the world to perish like an autumn leaf.
In a few days a new batch of juvenile convicts
filtered through Millbank, and after they were
safely lodged in their cells in the probationary
ward, they commenced, according to regula-
tions, the life of a convict.   Over each cell was
the name, age, crime, and sentence of the
prisoner.   I avoided any conflict with my
superiors, but most of them knew I had no
sympathy with the system of solitary confinement.   One afternoon Mr. Hepworth Dixon
and Mr. Charles Dickens called to see the
prison, and I had to show them over.   The
governor, chaplain, and deputy-governor were
holiday-keeping.   Everything was clean and
orderly; every piece of iron was brightened up
like silver, and you could eat off the floors.
To a casual visitor the machinery was perfect,
but in those cells, which could be counted by
the little iron gratings in the blank wall, there
was pulsating a mass of human wretchedness,
the sepulchre of all earthly hopes.   We had a
pleasant conversation, and they asked me to
their hotel in the evening, and we had a long
talk.   Mr. Dickens asked me to write my

opinions and experiences and send them to him in confidence. I had already published in a local paper several articles on the subject, which I collected and forwarded, with additional matter as to the average cost of each prisoner, the uselessness of some of their occupations, the unsuitable character of sedentary work, the feebleness of religious instruction, and other information which could be obtained by access to the prison books, which were of course at my command. I had no idea of anything being paid for by public money being private, especially the cost of a convict. Mr. Dickens wrote thanking me and asking for more information on one or two matters, which I supplied. Everything went on as usual. Weeks passed and I heard nothing; but one morning the chaplain told me a very unpleasant duty had fallen on him and the governor wished to see me at ten. I went into his office and saw a number of newspaper cuttings on the table. In a few minutes the deputy-governor and doctor came in, then another who was a stranger, and they formed a committee of

inquiry. The governor was in full uniform.
Suspicion naturally fell on me, because I had
made no secret of my opinions, which were
similar to those expressed in the cuttings.
After a little small talk from the chaplain, who
by this time I thoroughly disliked, about the
painfulness of the duty they had been instructed
by the Home Office to perform, he asked me
if I knew anything or had supplied any one
with the information contained in these cuttings, which he read out. I replied that I did
not recognise in him or any one the right to
ask of me such questions. The governor asked
me to give up my key, which was equivalent
to suspension for further inquiries. I wrote at
once to the principal and the gentleman who
had recommended me and told them I had
supplied the information, and they both advised
me to send in my resignation, which I did.

In a few days I received another letter from
the principal, requesting me to return to the
training Institution as soon as possible. I made
arrangements to leave, and after two years I
turned my back on a convict prison. Shortly
after I left the convicts mutinied and set fire

to the prison, and a good part of it was burned
down.   There was another inquiry, when the
discipline department broke down, and as time
went on many of my views were adopted, and
the treatment and discipline became more
rational.

One day, some years after, I was talking at
the corner of a street in Hull with some gentlemen who had come to the Yorkshire meeting.
Not far off was a group of ill-looking men; two
or three of them recognised me in a rather
familiar manner, and as soon as the gentlemen
moved off they came up and asked how I was.
I said, "I don't know you."   "Oh, don't you
remember 606 and 543?" two boys I had seen
on the convict-ship fifteen years before.   I
said, "What are you doing now?"   They
replied, "The same old game.   It pays better
than work."

I expected on my arrival at the training
Institution to have what was known among the
students as a "jawbation," but the Principal
received me kindly and gave a partial approval
of my views on prison discipline.   He said Mr.
Hepworth Dixon had called on him and told
him that there was nothing against me, that I

was well respected and, except among the rigid disciplinarians, much liked, but for the sake of discipline it was necessary to stop the adverse criticisms which had been published in the papers. Mr. Meyer, the science teacher, was ill; I took his work and confined my reading almost exclusively to the subjects I had to teach. After a few weeks it was evident Mr. Meyer would never return, but who would succeed him? The Government inspector, who had held a science professorship, recommended me, and I obtained the appointment, which I hoped might be a stepping-stone to something better. Considering the material I had to work upon my teaching was always reported on as good, and if my mathematics had been equal to my experimental knowledge I should have been a stronger man. I was now permanently and comfortably placed, and the work was agreeable to my taste. I was fond of it, and it was growing more popular as a part of education. I could not understand a teacher being educated who could not explain the construction and operation of a common pump, or the formulæ for common salts. I used to teach these things to convicts in my lessons on the common things, and the idea of men going out to teach others ignorant of science was to my mind a fraud.

The then Prime Minister had a small school in the country which had been endowed by his father, chiefly for providing a place for an old tutor of the family. This school was very unsatisfactory; it was held in a club-room connected with a public-house, whose sign bore the arms of the family, and when the wicket was drawn aside you could see all the mugs and beer barrels from the schoolroom. Very few boys attended, and those that did attend went more for their clothes than for learning. The master was never weary in telling you that it was entirely due to his teaching that we had a Prime Minister superior to Pitt. On his arrival in the morning, which was very uncertain, one boy was sent for hot water, another for a towel and soap, and after he had performed his toilet the boys stood round the desk and declined Latin nouns and translated exercises from Henry's First Book. At one of the annual examinations the Prime Minister had a party at his house, and he and several others, two of whom were Cabinet Ministers, were present at the examination. The wicket was open and the Chancellor of the Exchequer called out, "This is not a school, Sir Robert— it is a public-house." He replied, "I am going to build a new school." The boys showed their arithmetic books, which were poor, the Latin exercises useless, the writing all flourishes. Sir Robert took one of the copybooks, put on his gold spectacles, and said, "Let me give you a little advice: good writing does not require ornamentation, and bad writing is not worth it." Sir Robert knew the school was no good; a few tradesmen's sons went, who, but for their pride, could have obtained a better education at the National school. After the examination I had a long interview with the Prime Minister at his country house. I felt at first a little nervous; I had heard violent speeches against his policy, but I had never uttered a sentence against him myself. He proposed building a new school, pensioning the old master on his full salary, and establishing a good middle-class school in place of the grammar school founded by his father, where the sciences relating to agriculture and the mechanical trades should be taught.

With a view of favourably impressing the townspeople, he wished me to expend about fifty pounds in apparatus, which was to be publicly exhibited in the town hall, and I was to explain its uses and the industrial objects of this novel departure from old educational subjects. I suggested that if I could pick out a dozen boys from the elementary schools, I could give them lessons in the presence of their parents, and show them that this kind of teaching was not difficult and had important industrial uses. He thought it a good idea, and left me to work it out. An accident to Sir Robert, which terminated in his death, put an end to the project. I was disappointed, because I lost a rare opportunity of showing what I could do with what the papers called the New Education. I went to two other places with the same object; but the notion was in advance of its time, and there was no public response to the effort.

To have had an interview with the Prime Minister on education raised me in the estimation of the students. I was now making a fair income, and I thought of getting married. I mentioned the matter to the Principal, who saw no objection; he thought it gave me a better standing; and so I got married, and I had no cause to regret it, and it was not a failure. But my affection for my wife attained its climax when, after forty years, I stood, with my five grown-up children, by her grave. Before we were married we had to find a house. Our income was small, and we had to be modest in our rent. After going about within a mile radius of my work, we settled on a compo. thing called a villa. I hated it, but my future wife thought it would do very nicely, as all future wives do. I was only reconciled to it because it was in a muddy lane, surrounded by cabbage gardens and orchards, and on a spring evening I could sit in a little garden, not much larger than the house, and scent the hawthorn and lilac and hear the cuckoo. The house was a wretched, jerry-built affair, and gave us no end of trouble and expense.

In addition to my teaching at the Institution I had a good deal of teaching at other places. At one school the lady hoped I should be able in future to give my lessons without any diagrams of the inside of animals. Everything was going on pleasantly, when I saw in the paper that the Principal had accepted a colonial bishopric, and unless the vice-principal succeeded, this meant a revolution in the place. Everything was disorganised until the council appointed a new Principal, and, to the general regret of all the masters, the vice-Principal, who had been there from the beginning, was passed over in favour of one who had more influence and less experience. The vice-Principal resigned, and the new Principal obtained the appointment for an intimate friend, who said ditto to the Principal. Things now began to grow very unpleasant. There was constant friction between the old masters and Principal. Fault was found with their teaching; the workshops and printing-press were abandoned as fads, the tools and type sold; and it was evident that the old masters would have to go and make room for others appointed through the recommendation of the Principal. The first attacked was the master of method, who had a more independent position than the others. It was said that he held sceptical opinions; that he had been seen coming out of a Unitarian chapel; that the books in his library were such as ought not to be read; and things were made so uncomfortable that he resigned; and he was succeeded by one of the most contemptible, hypocritical, lying creatures that ever walked on two legs. Everything he heard—and things he never heard, but invented—he retailed to the Principal, to the prejudice of some of the students and old masters. He used to watch on Saturday afternoons to see where they went; he used to crawl about the passages after the lights were out, to hear what the students talked about. The Principal, to his disgrace, lent a greedy ear to his stories, and drank with pleasure the most fulsome flattery. This creature was married, and carried on a clandestine correspondence with the housekeeper!

One day I was copying letters in an adjoining room, and, as the door was partly open, I heard his conversation with the Principal about one of the students, and the questions were such as no pure-minded man would have put or answered. They had no idea I was in the room, and I left quietly without their knowing it. The student, I believe, was a pure-minded young man. He was not brilliant, but there was a prejudice against him. He had been seen with a young woman, whom I knew to be his sister; but this oily-tongued creature, instead of defending him, actually aggravated his offence by saying he had often seen them come out of public-houses together under suspicious circumstances, which I knew to be false. Within an hour I saw him talking to this young man, and after he was gone I asked him what they had been talking about. I saw he was rather sorrowful. He told me that this hypocrite had been interceding with the Principal on his behalf until things became very unpleasant; but the Principal had determined to send him down, not on any specific charge, but vague insinuations, which have sent more men to the devil than criminal charges. If you wish to ruin a man, shrug your shoulders when his name is mentioned, and put on a knowing expression without making any charge; this will succeed better than any definite accusation of wrong-doing.

I was obliged to eat my food at the same table. The vice-Principal took the head of the table—he was a clergyman, after the Principal's own heart—with this creature on his right. When he spoke to a female teacher he used to put his arms round her and express his fatherly affection for her temporal and spiritual welfare and a good report from her Majesty's inspector. When the *Non Nobis Domine* was sung he turned up the whites of his eyes. He used to tell us how he had risen before daybreak to read St. Chrysostom and other Fathers in the original, when I knew—and everybody knew—that he was unable to translate correctly a simple sentence in the Delectus. All this was received at the table with wonder and admiration, chiefly from the artful way in which he used to tell the story. His mouth opened like a crocodile's, and he ate and drank like a pig. I have had serious differences with men, but I hated this man. When I saw him walking about in clerical black and a white choker, with his hands under the tails of his coat, I felt what joy there would be if I could only kick him. His great recommendation for model master was his sound views on all Church matters.

One master after another resigned, until I was the only one left, and I felt my days were numbered.

I had one or two friends on the Council, but constant reports were made that the efficient government of the college was impossible so long as any of the old masters remained. However unfounded or unjust these reports were, you could have no chance when the Principal advised the Council. Disagreeable and extra duties were imposed upon me, which, as a married man, were often impossible, and which I refused to perform. This brought me into direct conflict with the Council and Principal, and our interviews were very unpleasant. He accused me of keeping company with a gipsy, of once obtaining my livelihood as a political agitator, of selling a shovel, not attending church, and stirring up a spirit of insubordination among the students. I knew who prompted these accusations—the man I abhorred was a genius at this work. In my anger I said, " If you repeat these accusations, I will strike you." I walked out of the library, wrote for my salary, and never set foot in the place again. When, years after, I was ordered to visit the Institution officially, I excused myself on the ground of my former connection. I am free to confess that I could not have trusted myself to act justly. A few of the students privately presented me with a testimonial, but it was a sore trial for me. A good part of my income was gone; I had a wife and child; I had made a bitter enemy of the man to whom I should be obliged to refer for another situation, and the prospect was not cheerful. The Principal had been for thirty years a Quaker, and had written tracts in defence of the doctrines of the Society of Friends; but when a man changes from a Quaker to something else, he becomes a tyrant and a bigot. His only claim to the principalship was not his learning or goodness of heart—for he had neither—but his sound views on Church matters.

CHAPTER XIV.

ABOUT this time some gentlemen were anxious to establish, not far from where I lived, a trade school ; not a school for teaching trades, as some imagined, but a school in which science and drawing in their application to the industrial arts were to form, with French, the principal part of the teaching. The fees were low, so as not to exclude the humbler middle and mechanic class from an education which could not be obtained either in the elementary school or the grammar school, and which was thought likely to be of more service than either. There was a committee, of whom six were Fellows of the Royal Society. The chairman, who was a clergyman, was also a Fellow. There was a resident headmaster, who had to teach ordinary subjects ; a science master, an art master, and a French master. These were to attend two or three days a week. I applied for the science mastership, and obtained it.

The school opened with nearly a hundred boys. I threw myself, as did the other masters, earnestly into the experiment. We resolved that if the thing failed it should not be our fault. I cultivated as far as I could the good opinion and friendship of the boys and their parents. The secretary informed me that the committee who used to visit the school were much pleased with the success of our teaching. In three months the boys had learned the symbols and combining equivalents of the commonly occurring elementary bodies, and could perform simple experiments.

One afternoon I had a note saying the chairman wished to see me. When I called on him I could see there was something which troubled him. We had been on the most friendly terms, but he now appeared reserved and doubtful. Our views on educational questions were the same. He said: " The other day the Principal of the training college called on me, and, although we only live a walking distance from each other, he has never called before, although he frequently passes my house. I don't want to make you unhappy, but I think it my duty to tell you he is no friend of yours, and if I believed a tithe of what he came to tell me I should feel it my duty to ask you to resign. But I shall do nothing of the kind, because I think a person in his position, calling himself a Christian minister, to come unasked to do an injury to another is as bad in him or worse than anything he told me about you. I asked him if he would write down what he had said, so that I could submit it to the committee, but this he declined to do, and I told him unless he did I should take no further notice of the matter." Just at that moment his wife came into the library, where we were sitting, and said, "James, I think as soon as he began talking to the injury of one of our trade school teachers you should have ordered him to leave. I felt inclined to do so, because I saw through him at once." The chairman said, "What has occurred will not pass out of this room, but I thought you ought to know it, that you may in future be on your guard." He said, "I want no explanation, and I hope you will try, as I shall, to forget it."

We worked together most amicably for three or four years, and when he removed into the country I used to visit him, and these visits were of the most pleasurable kind. They continued until I saw the green turf over his grave in a little country churchyard near where I was born. My connection with the trade school brought me into contact with some of the advanced educationists of the time, and at educational meetings and conferences I was pretty well known.

About this time the Board of Trade was endeavouring to formulate a scheme for trade and navigation schools, and for these schools masters were to be trained at the School of Mines. Six scholarships of thirty shillings a week were offered, and I was advised to try for one of them, which I fortunately obtained. I was now obliged to attend at least three days a week from ten till four, and, as I lived nearly five miles from the school and walked backwards and forwards, I had enough to do, especially during the winter, to keep up my attendances. I was also busily engaged in teaching in the evening at the Trade and Navigation Schools at Poplar, and I had also large classes at the Polytechnic, which I continued teaching until the fatal accident occurred by the fall of the stone staircase.

There was drawing nearer and nearer an examination upon which the loss or renewal of my scholarship, with an extra five shillings a week, depended. Of all the cruel inventions of man for the mental torture of his fellow-creatures nothing is equal to a competitive examination, especially when his future existence depends on the result. The prospects of a prison cell to an innocent man is more cheerful than a competitive examination. The teachers at the School of Mines were the most distinguished men in the subjects they had to teach, except the chemistry professor. They were all professors, and examined us in the Universities, and what I and others knew, compared with what they knew, was not a very cheerful prospect. The most terrible man was the teacher of physics. There was a blackboard the area of the wall of a small room which moved up and down like a window, and in two minutes it was covered from top to bottom with x's and y's and formulæ which no one could read but himself. He was not a good teacher for students whose knowledge of science was only elementary, and when he tried to explain the simplest problem about the pressure of fluids or the like, which could have been done by experiment, he at once went to the blackboard. He used to say, "I will deal with this problem so that you can all understand it," but none of us did understand it. He spared no trouble, and was sincerely anxious about our progress, but he was no teacher for men of our attainments. We all respected him and applauded him when he began, and particularly when he finished. We had a profound regard for his books, which none of us could read beyond the title-page. I felt pretty safe about the chemistry, but nervous about the physics. I devoted every spare minute to the subject, because failure in one subject meant failure in all. I used to carry about little problems on a card, and study them in the train or anywhere—much may be done this way—but, as it often happens, none of these problems came in at the examination.

The day before the examination was a dreadful day. My wife was ill in bed, the girl had gone out, and I had to take care of the child to prevent its falling into the fire or eating cinders. At the same time I had to read up for the next day's examination, which lasted for several hours. As only five were examined, the results were published the following day. I was afraid to go into the library to look at the paper—the fear was terrible. At last I heard that only two had passed, and I was one of them. My joy knew no bounds. I forgot my companions. I ran home as if I had no gravity. I seemed to swim through the air, because it was my first severe examination. I went through my chemistry, and the examiner complimented me, and when he was removed to Berlin he invited me to visit him. A married man should hesitate about examinations; if he fails before he is married, he is not likely to succeed after. Every young man should strive to get behind his examinations as quickly as possible.

My work now went on comfortably. I had plenty of teaching, and was in the receipt of an income to which I adapted my wants. After nearly two years I passed my final examinations, obtained my certificates from the Board of Trade, which I now have in my room, and was ready for an appointment, but no appointment offered. The scheme was in advance of the time. My scholarship was continued for another year. The trade school at which I taught was closed. Repeated efforts had been made in vain to obtain pecuniary assistance from the Education Office. It was not to be expected that year after year men would continue heavy subscriptions towards a school which they thought worthy of help from the Education Office. One hundred and twenty boys had to find their way back to elementary schools or cheap middle-class schools.

I had a good friend, to whom I shall ever feel grateful, who obtained for me an appointment, which had the prospect of permanency, in one of the education departments of the Government. As soon as this was known my friend the reverend the Principal turned up. He called on my patron and repeated the insinuations and scandals of two years before. When my patron mentioned it to me he said it was very serious, and he was very sorry. Fortunately, the chairman of the trade school committee, who was a great educationist and a well-known scientific man, was an intimate friend of my patron. I lost no time in communicating to him what had occurred. The next morning he had an interview with my patron and the heads of the department, and from that time I was at peace.

In a few weeks I met the reverend the gentleman in a narrow street. The temptation was too strong—how I hated him! I went up to him and spoke my mind very freely: " You black crawling creature, you have tried to take the bread out of my children's mouths and you have failed." He turned as pale as death, he thought I was about to strike him, but I knew better; he tried to call the police, but his voice failed him. This, thank God, was our final interview.

The other model creature went on and prospered for a time because he was a genius in his art. The archbishop gave him a degree without examination; he was ordained and obtained the appointment of Principal to a mixed training college. He was received by the committee as a kind of superior angel. They were indeed most fortunate in securing such a man, but very soon some began to have doubts as to his angelic character. In a mixed training college, where both sexes

have to meet at an impressionable age,
it is impossible to prevent eyes looking
love to eyes, but this was a sin of the
deepest dye among young people, and had
to be constantly checked, although it is the
strongest impulse of human nature.   But
watch it as you will you will never prevent it.
There is intense pleasure in loving one
another without even saying so, and it so
happened that an affectionate weakness
sprang up between a young man and a young
woman in the training college.   The eye of
the Principal saw it; he talked privately to the
young man and woman in the most affectionate and fatherly spirit, and on her leaving
kissed her, and as they were shortly to take
charge of schools he thought it better for
example's sake that they should not speak or
take notice of each other in the college.
Occasionally he would allow them an evening
out.   Could anything be more kind or con-
siderate ?   Would not these young people
have given up their lives for the good-natured
Principal, who knew their hearts' longing ?
After the examination they left and went to

different schools, and when the Government inspector visited the training college the reverend the Principal wished him to say to these two artless, innocent young people when he visited their schools that he was sorry to hear unpleasant rumours as to their moral conduct at the training college.

The girl's school was first visited, and when he mentioned the matter the young woman cried and was naturally indignant, demanded his authority, which he was under a promise not to give. She wrote to her young man, and he wrote to the office, and the matter being pressed now became the subject of official inquiry. The inspector was obliged to give his authority, and now what happened ? The reverend the Principal denied ever giving them permission to go out together, they had gone out clandestinely without his authority, and it resolved itself into a question of truth between the parties. Lying requires the constant invention of other lies, so he denied saying anything to the inspector, or suggesting anything which reflected on the moral conduct of these young people. The authorities satisfied themselves who was the liar, and requested the committee to call for his resignation, which they at first refused. They had held an inquiry, which had established his innocence. "You retain your Principal and we withdraw our grants," was the department's reply. No public department would have come to this decision without full justification.

He now became incumbent of a small Episcopal chapel, but he had not been there long before the same scandalmongering began among his congregation, which ended in his removal. I was one day walking with the chief magistrate, when I caught sight of this creature. The Provost asked, "Do you know that man? he is a countryman of yours and would be glad of half a crown." I made no reply, my heart softened and I forgave him. I had been taught by one of the professors at the School of Mines that there could be no infringement of any physical or moral law without corresponding suffering and punishment, and although the moral law is more complex and difficult to understand, yet there seemed in the life of this man a just retributive punishment. The deceit upon which he lived grew weaker and at last failed. The men who stood by me in the hour of trial will ever be remembered with gratitude. To them I owe thirty years of a fairly prosperous and successful life; that I had faults I admit, and my manner was not always agreeable, and some of my troubles might have been avoided by more prudence. If I disliked any one they knew it without my saying so. Most natures are open to flattery, but I hated it. If, as a friend once said to me, you had only taken half the trouble to manage these fellows as you take to convince them, you might have done anything with them. But my nature recoiled at the idea of praising a man for his intellect when I thought him an idiot; others might do it but I never could.

CHAPTER XV.

I WAS sitting quietly one evening with my family after a hard day's teaching, which is the hardest of all work, when two gravel diggers from the common wished to see me.

They came to tell me that they were born in the parish and had been gravel diggers for years, and their fathers before them. They had no gardens or allotments; but had planted a few rows of potatoes on an exhausted part of the pit, and just as they appeared above ground a gentleman who called himself the lessee, and who had recently added six acres of the common to his own private grounds, came with two men and levelled their crop of potatoes, and told them if they did it again he should have them up. They had come to ask my advice. My first impulse was to go with these men and break down his fence; I felt so angry that, had I been single, I was prepared to risk the consequences, but it was of no use sacrificing a wife and family in what I then believed to be the assertion of a right. If I had succeeded I should have been crowned with laurels; if I had failed, as I probably should, the public would have called me a fool, and would have allowed me to go to prison and my wife and family to the union.

De Lolme says for every wrong or grievance

there is a constitutional remedy, but I could
not see where the constitution came in to
preserve the common. I saw, what everybody
saw, that the common was fast melting away.
Private owners adjoining the common were
constantly making improvements by adding
portions of the common to their own property.
The railways had enclosed acres not required
or provided for in these acts, and in time this
surplus was divided among their head officials.
Six acres were enclosed for a telescope which
was never put up, speculating builders
turned a greedy eye on what remained, and
here and there, like the scouts of an army,
things called villas sprang up like mushroons.
The tallest and ugliest production of compo.
and rotten bricks at the corner of each street
were intended for public-houses. The common
was threatened on every side, and the increasing army of landgrabbers and jerry - builders
would soon have joined hands on the last
square foot of turf, and one of the most lovely
commons within a few miles of Charing Cross
would have become a wilderness of bricks and
chimney-pots.

We were told there was no remedy. The gravelpits were filled up with garbage and rubbish for the foundations of eligible villas and ground-rents. All these enclosures were no doubt made with the formal sanction of the lord of the manor on the representation of his agents, and as the common was for the most part surrounded by poor inhabitants there was no money for litigation, the only cheap comfort was to grumble. The adjacent common was, on the other hand, surrounded by rich merchants and bankers with large houses and grounds, and any attempt on the common even for railways was threatened with a powerful resistance. I was unable to help these poor potato men, but it occurred to me that a letter to the newspapers might attract attention. I wrote three letters to the daily papers. Only one, the *Standard*, inserted the letter, but this was sufficient; other letters followed, and there was evidently a strong-growing public sentiment against the further enclosure of commons near London. A public meeting was held in each of the parishes ad-joining the common, and resolutions were passed, but still the enclosures went on. Some suggested an injunction to prevent building, but we were advised that no one but a copyholder could bring the action and claim the relief, and the few copyholders left were under obligation or at the mercy of the agents of the lord of the manor. These copyholders were asked to become plaintiffs, but with one consent they all began to make excuses : the public had no common rights.

During the summer we held large open-air meetings and collected money for the coming fight. We went to neighbouring parishes in a waggon drawn by a pair of horses and held open-air meetings.

Public interest and enthusiasm were created which extended to other parts of the metropolis. The agitation, which began with the labouring and some of the middle classes, gradually extended to others of greater wealth and influence, until at last we had a powerful and wealthy committee. A gentleman in the neighbourhood whom I had opposed at elections became a close friend on this question, and he offered to put five hundred or a thousand pounds in the bank, if we could raise a corresponding sum, and become plaintiff. We raised a large fund, and then discovered he had no standing as plaintiff. As soon as we had money the lawyers came to us with advice. We petitioned the House of Commons, we sent deputations to the District Board, we memoralised the Metropolitan Board until at last they insulted us and refused to see us. After some difficulty we obtained an interview with the lord of the manor, and after discussing the matter in the presence of his agents and lawyers he asked, " Do you question my right to dispose of the common? " All the other members of the deputation were dumb. I waited to hear what they would say, but as no one spoke I replied, " I am sorry to say, my lord, that we do question your right." He turned on his heel, his lawyers followed, and we were shown the door by his footman.

No sooner were we outside than the other members of the deputation turned on me and said I had greatly offended his lordship and destroyed all hopes of a settlement, and yet the question of right was the great question at all our meetings. I began to grow sick and weary of deputations, and I loathed the Metropolitan Board, because they led us to expect an Act of Parliament. I wrote a respectful letter to the lord of the manor, pointing out the importance of what was left of the common for health and recreation, and reminded him that these privileges had been enjoyed undisputed, in the language of lawyers, from the time " whereof the memory of man faileth not." This brought back a rough letter about agitation and rights of property. I sent my letter with his lordship's reply to the *Times*, which brought a very angry letter back saying the letter was not intended for publication ; to which I replied that it was not marked private, and I felt the subject was of too much public importance to be dealt with privately. I had reason to believe that his lordship had been kept in ignorance of the facts by his agents and lawyers, who had represented me as a demagogue and attributing to me language which I should never dream of using; but give a lie a few hours' start and it is impossible to overtake it.

After the interview with the lord of the manor it was decided to hold a mass-meeting on the common. It had been hinted in some of the papers that the only way of bringing the matter to an issue was to destroy the fences and knock down the houses. The impression had got abroad that something of this kind was intended at the meeting, which was to be held in the last enclosure. The Commissioner of Police sent about a hundred policemen, who were hidden behind trees and furze bushes. The waggon was placed in position near the last enclosure. We had an informal meeting of a few of the committee, and when we saw the men assembling in large numbers armed with pickaxes, sledge-hammers, crow-bars, and saws, some of the committee thought it would be better not to hold any meeting, and they left. I was in the waggon with only two others out of twenty. The inspector of police was riding backwards and forwards like a general on a field-day. He rode up to the waggon and said he had been instructed by the Commissioner of Police to deliver to some one a letter. I read the letter, which was to the effect that I should be held responsible for any unnecessary destruction of property, but the removal of one or two rails, to raise the question of right, would not be resisted.

I knew the removal of one or two rails in the presence of some hundreds of armed and excited men, who were calling out " Give us the order to begin ! " could only end in disaster and riot.   I saw the peril of the situation, and made a speech in which I pointed out that this wholesale and retail robbery of the common had been made by rich men who had acres of their own.   I mentioned the potato incident, and that the right of land-owners to land which had not yet been dis-puted would be disputed if they laid claim to the commons.   Property in land was subject to the will of the State expressed through the people.   I have always fought what I believed to be the battle of the poor and the oppressed, and I begged and entreated of them to go home quietly and avoid the public-house. Any conflict with the police would ruin our cause and destroy all hope of success.   They all retired peaceably, and when everything was quiet the police went home without any engagement.

I had acquired considerable influence over the men by my deep sympathy with their loss of the common. The lot of a poor labourer is often a very hard lot, but public opinion was growing in our favour. The newspapers began to report meetings and write favourable articles. We approached the Lord Mayor, held a meeting at the Mansion House, and collected nearly two hundred pounds. The late Mr. Fawcett, Sir Charles Dilke, and others gave us valuable help. The agitation had now reached a higher level; but we were still helpless and no nearer our object, and now and then fresh enclosures were made. We published a large map of the common as it was in 1820 and as it was in 1865, showing the enclosures, with the names of the men who made them and, as far as we knew, what they paid for them. Land not worth half a crown an acre for agricultural purposes was now worth a thousand pounds an acre for building, and this increased value was entirely due not to the lord of the manor, but to the growth of population.

A footpath which ran diagonally across a piece of the common was stopped at both ends, and the land added to the gardens of adjoining owners. This enclosure deprived the public of a convenient footpath, and stopping it created much ill-feeling and indignation. The enclosure was protected at both ends with a high closed fence of a most formidable character, lined inside and out with sheet-iron. The one boundary was the railway, and the other the gardens of the common-stealers. Men would assemble in small detachments in the evening and look at the fence. The police were on the lookout. They expected a siege some evening, and they were not disappointed.

One evening about a dozen men came out of a near public-house and with heavy hammers and stones attacked the fence at both ends, broke it down, trampled down the fruit-trees, and went out at the other end amid the deafening cheers of a large crowd which had by this time come together. One stupid young fellow, who had recently come up from the country to work in the gardens, took up a large stone and deliberately knocked down some palings. His companions saw the police and called him away, but he was deaf, and the police took him into custody, and he was locked up. I happened, fortunately for myself, to be away, but, unfortunately for the young man, the whole affair was so sudden and unexpected that no arrangements were made to defend him. The next morning he was brought before the magistrate, confessed his guilt, and expressed his sorrow. He was sentenced to a fortnight's imprisonment. The common-stealers pleaded damage and pressed for a heavy punishment as an example. If instead of pleading guilty he had pleaded a right, the magistrate must have dismissed the case.

On my return I called on his employer, who expressed his willingness to give the man work when he came out of prison. I at once prepared a memorial to the Home Secretary for his liberation. I first went to the parson of our district and asked him to sign it. Now this man, who had often expressed to me his full sympathy with our efforts, began to make all sorts of excuses. The common-stealers formed part of his congregation. They were wealthy and subscribed liberally to his church, and unless they first signèd it he could not without giving offence. This was the representative of the Church of the poor man, which ought to have protected him against the greed and avarice of the rich. I should never have gone to him but for his frequent private expressions of approval and encouragement. I placed a table in front of a shop where hundreds of persons passed daily to the railway, and in the course of two days obtained nearly a thousand signatures. I took the memorial at once to the House of Commons and sent for Mr. Fawcett, who was out. I then sent for Sir Charles Dilke, who suggested I should leave it at the Home Office. I knew what would become of it if it found its way to the Home Office. It would probably be referred to every person, from the messenger to the Assistant Secretary, who would refer it from one to the other, whose business would be to initial it, write on, " Seen—refer to Brown—look up precedents,"

"Refer to Asst. Sec. for instructions," "Refer to committing magistrate"; and before all was finished the young man would have done his time. I pressed Sir Charles Dilke to take it direct to the Home Secretary, who was in the House, and explain the circumstances of the case and its urgency. I called next day at the Office and found that the matter had been referred to the committing magistrate, who offered no objection to the prisoner's release, and I expected in a day or two the governor of the prison would receive an order accordingly. But no order came. I called again at the Home Office, and was informed that the papers had been forwarded to Balmoral. I waited two or three days, when I was informed there had been some mistake, and the papers would be returned to Balmoral at once. After the young man had served his term of imprisonment all but two days, the governor received an order for his release.

A few days after his imprisonment his poor mother came up from Suffolk in great sorrow and went direct to the police-station, where she was informed by somebody, which everybody denied, that I was the cause of her son's imprisonment. I was deeply grieved when she came to my house, and her sorrow was the sorrow of a mother. I gave her some tea, made her comfortable, and lodged her for the night. I sent for the treasurer of the Common Fund, and we sent her home with the assurance that her son would not suffer or lose his character. She was much hurt when she applied at the prison to see her son. The door was slammed in her face, and she was rudely told to be off about her business. A person in distress is more sensible of kindness than those who have never tasted the waters of deep sorrow through the errors of their children. When his companions heard of his release they procured a van and decorated it with ribbons, laurels, evergreens, and flowers. An arm-chair was placed in the centre for the prisoner. A band of music arrived at the prison gates, and the prisoner was received with hearty expressions of sympathy and goodwill. The band, with van and pro- cession, moved slowly to the scene of the late battle, for which the young man had suffered ten days' imprisonment. The procession stopped as long as the police permitted it in front of the houses of the common-stealers and played, almost to the bursting of their instruments, "See the conquering hero comes," with occasional yells of "Who stole the common?" The procession moved through the parish to the schoolroom, where I presented the prisoner with a new suit of clothes and five pounds, provided by the committee. I persuaded the audience to go quietly home. I sent two men with the prisoner to his lodgings. Some of the men had been drinking and were getting noisy and troublesome, and when they are in that state you may as well try to persuade a milestone to go home. I did all I could, and as the young man was safe I left the others, and the next morning two or three of them were fined five shillings each.

Our first battle began and ended in a police-court. But there was a still more formidable battle preparing. Writs were served on two or three persons for damage and trespass in asserting their right to the footpath. Evidence of user, as shown by old maps and deaf old men and women over eighty years of age, had to be collected. After some weeks we arrived at the assizes before the Lord Chief Justice. We had great difficulty in keeping, day after day, thirty-three witnesses together; they would wander all over the town, and the old men would be sitting on doorsteps smoking with a strip of blue ribbon in their hats. When our case came on there was a good deal of preliminary sparring between counsel. At last they got into the ring. When the defence came the judge seemed restless; he constantly interrupted our counsel, who was the son of a judge, and shortly after himself became a judge. I was sitting near him (the counsel), and I could see the blood rising in his neck like mercury in a thermometer, until at last it came to boiling heat. He pulled himself together and said, " There must be something in my manner exceedingly offensive to your lordship of which I am not conscious, or I should not be interrupted in this way." "Oh dear no! pray go on."

And the case, which threatened at the beginning of the defence to be finished in ten minutes, went on for a day and a half, and ended with a verdict for the plaintiffs. The judge told the jury there was no footpath across a common. We appealed and lost. We had a meeting for mutual condolence.

We were advised unless we could secure a copyholder, of which there were not more than six left, or an Act of Parliament, the common must go. I managed to obtain a list of copyholders, and there was only one at all likely to become a plaintiff. He was a poor, ignorant old man, either a bachelor or a widower, living in a dirty, tumble-down, pantiled old copyhold, and obtained a miserable living by selling potatoes, brickdust, and treacle. I had often seen him, but had never spoken to him. I mentioned these qualifications to the lawyer, who said, " He is the very man ! " I made some private inquiries, and found he had a weakness for gin and water. I passed his shop almost every morning about the time he was watering his greens and sorting his potatoes. The next

time I said, "Good morning, Mr. Wrigsby."
He returned the compliment. I praised his
potatoes and at once ordered half a bushel.
I allowed a few mornings to pass by, simply
wishing him good morning. I said, "If you
will call on me in the evening and bring up
another half-bushel of potatoes I will pay
you." He came up. I sent my wife into
another room and asked Mr. Wrigsby to have
a pipe. He sat down. I ordered some hot
gin and water. We talked about the rates
and taxes, and we agreed that the parish was
going to the bad. I asked, "Who is your
landlord ? "   He replied, " Nobody ; it's
copyhold. One gentleman endeavoured to
purchase a copyhold, but he would not
have been admitted by the Court Leet."

I said, "You are a copyholder?"

He replied : "Yes, but I never go to the
Court. My father was a copyholder, and he
kept two cows and a pony on the common, but
I have no cows, and I am my own pony, and
think it would be a good thing if the common
was built over; it would bring a little more
business into the parish."

22

" Have a little more gin and water, Mr. Wrigsby. I think as you don't get any benefit from the common the least they could have done would have been to give you compensation, or a piece of the common. You are a poor, hard-working man, and I think they have behaved very badly to you. All the rich people round the common have been helping themselves pretty freely, and I daresay you know I have been doing what I can to stop any further stealing."

" Everybody in the parish knows what you have done, but you don't seem to have prevented it. I hear that fellow Dobs, who owes me a bill I can't get, is taking in a bit near the lane."

" Mr. Wrigsby, Dobs is a land-stealer, and you are the only man in the parish that can stop his stealing."

" How can I stop it? I have no money to go to law."

" Mr. Wrigsby, you would be the greatest benefactor this parish ever had if you would only enter your protest against this robbery of your rights. I will guarantee that you shall not be sixpence the poorer, and if we win you may be richer."

"Do you want me to go before the magistrate and complain?"

"No. I want you to sign a paper that you object to these enclosures."

"Well, as it's to oblige you, I don't mind, if you will promise to stand by me, but I can't afford any expense, and I depends on you. If the common was built over it might not do me much good. I daresay they would build shops as sells the same as I do."

"When shall we meet to sign this paper? Will you come to my house, or shall I come to yours?"

"Just as you like."

"Then, if you don't mind, perhaps you will come to me next Thursday evening at half-past six. You need not mention to any one our conversation, because it only concerns the copyholders, and you are almost the only one left. Will you have a little more refreshment before you go home?"

"No, thank you."

As soon as I saw Mr. Wrigsby's back I ran

off to the lawyer and reported our interview.
He was highly delighted. He said, "At
seven my clerk shall be there with the plaint ;
it has been prepared a long time. You and
my clerk must witness the signature."

On Thursday Mr. Wrigsby was in good
time. I had ready the long clay and tobacco
and gin and water. We talked about parish
matters, and just as the first glass was finished
I heard a knock at the door. I said, "I daresay this is the man with the paper." It was
important that Wrigsby should have his wits
about him. The clerk began reading the
plaint, and I kept Mr. Wrigsby occupied in
conversation while the rights of estuary and
turbary were gone over. Mr. Wrigsby paid
little attention to it. He made no remarks,
except asking if all that writing was about the
common. It was rather a long business, but
at last we came to the end, "whereof the
memory of man faileth not," and Mr. Wrigsby
signed it in the presence of two witnesses. I
shall never forget the expression of joy on the
clerk's countenance as he watched Mr.
Wrigsby put on his spectacles and sign his

name. He took a little piece of blotting out of his pocket and placed it carefully over the signatures, put the plaint in his black bag, said " Good-night, Mr. Wrigsby," and was out of the house in an instant.

Mr. Wrigsby wondered he should be in such a hurry. He thought he had come to talk about the common. Poor Mr. Wrigsby little thought that he had commenced proceedings against the lord of the manor, the Brighton and South Coast Railway Company, the West London Extension, the South-Western, and six others. It may be said that I ought not to have taken advantage of Mr. Wrigsby's weakness, but it was our last extremity, and Aristotle would have defended it. Whatever came of it, Mr. Wrigsby could not suffer; he had nothing to suffer with. The lawyer asked me to accompany him to a Q.C. in Lincoln's Inn, who was the best authority on real property. A few minutes after ten he came into his chambers, and the lawyer laid on his table the plaint. After some general remarks about commons he turned over page after page, then turned it back again, then looked at the signatures, and appeared to me not very sanguine about the matter. Anyhow, we were now going to law, and there was some satisfaction in knowing it. I ventured in the most respectful way to say, "I think, sir, I ought to tell you that the plaintiff in this case is a very illiterate man." "I should think he is a damned idiot, or he would never be a plaintiff in a case of this kind. There is no law on the subject—the law has to be made. I will attend to it, but God only knows where it will end."

We left, and for a few weeks everything was quiet. I occasionally called on Mr. Wrigsby, whom the lawyer had never seen, and what astonished me was that he had told this eminent Q.C. that he didn't want to see him. As soon as the other side knew Wrigsby was plaintiff, off they went to him, and told him that he would be sent to prison for signing an affidavit. He came to me in great trouble, and told me the enemy had been to him. I gave him a pipe and something to drink, and as we parted he said pathetically, "You will stand by me, won't you?" I replied, "To the very last." I frequently called on him with words of comfort and encouragement. At last he was cited to appear on his affidavit before the court, and immediately after he had an attack of gout, which I hoped would continue long enough for the case to stand over. I called on his doctor, and said, "I have seen Wrigsby. I don't think he is well enough to appear." He replied, "Don't you want him to appear? I can give you a certificate for the usual fee," which I paid, and Wrigsby did not appear. The Long Vacation was coming on, and Wrigsby still had the gout. The defendants were very anxious to force on the case, but were rather late. I hoped, and the committee hoped, something would happen. We continued at convenient intervals our meetings, and public feeling and most of the newspapers were with us, but they could not stop the lawsuit or say much about it. One paper praised the public spirit and intelligence of the plaintiff.

As soon as the courts opened Wrigsby had to appear. The doctor's certificate had lost its virtue. I saw him, and explained to him that, no matter what they asked, he was to

say that he was a copyholder, and meant to
protect his rights. He repeated this over
to me. I begged of him not to say anything
more. I said, " If they ask you your age say
you are a copyholder." I called with a cab
for the great plaintiff, but I had my fears. I
felt as if we were going to an execution, but
Wrigsby knew he was going into society, and
dressed accordingly. He had on a pair of
primrose-coloured breeches and gaiters, which
hung on his body in graceful fulness ; a yellow
plush waistcoat, with large glass buttons,
which gleamed like cat's eyes ; a blue coat,
far too small, with a few brass buttons ; and a
large white choker twisted round his neck like
a tablecloth. The appearance of the plaintiff
in court was a sensation. Six defendants
were each separately represented by counsel,
supported by a strong detachment of lawyers.
Where the carcase is there will the eagles be
gathered together. As Mr. Wrigsby stood up
the Vice-Chancellor looked at him, as well he
might, for he was a natural curiosity. Counsel for the Railway Company began by a few
loving remarks about Mr. Wrigsby's health,

and in less than twenty minutes Wrigsby told
the whole story of his signing the affidavit—
what I had told him to say, that I would stick
to him to the last, that he should not be sixpence the poorer for the lawsuit, perhaps
better, that the common was no good to him
and never had been, and it was to oblige me
that he signed the paper. He didn't know
exactly what it was about, but I told him it was
all right. If an earthquake had swallowed up
me and the others I should not have objected.

After all my work this was a terrible blow.
The lawyer leaned over to me and said, " It is
all up." The counsel and lawyers for the
defendants sniggered at each other, waiting
for the magic words, " Judgment for defendants, with costs." The thieves who had
stolen the common laughed outright, and as
I came out of court jeered at me. The
Vice-Chancellor, a pious, good old man—may
he rest in peace !—said, " I shall reserve
judgment." Then the counsel and lawyers
stared at each other and leisurely packed up
a cartload of papers and books and left. I
never spoke to Wrigsby again, and I felt

counsel's opinion of him at our first joyful interview was correct. What was to be done? Another mass-meeting where we could pour out our sorrows and find comfort in the frantic hurrahs of the demos, who wanted to go at the fences! In a few days we heard rumours of an armistice. I never knew for certain; but I believe the good Vice-Chancellor had an interview with the lord of the manor, who consented to a friendly Act of Parliament by which all that was left of the common—about one hundred and fifty acres—should remain open and unenclosed for ever on payment of two hundred pounds a-year, or twenty years' purchase, secured on the rates of the parishes adjoining the common, which was about a farthing in the pound. The parishes cheerfully assented, and after five years the fighting ended.

The Metropolitan Board of Works employed counsel to oppose the Bill, and we were put to great expense by the opposition. We had to find the money for this struggle as best we could. But the Board of Works spent the ratepayers' money in resisting the Bill. A more unprincipled and unjustifiable act could only be explained by the rottenness and corruption of the body that promoted the opposition. Happily they failed.

During the whole of this agitation I was busily engaged in teaching. My domestic life was not improved by the constant service of writs at the instigation of common-stealers and speculating builders. At one time I had seven writs in the house, which were handed over to the solicitor for the committee. It was thought by some that I should have more weight if I had some official position in the parish, and I was elected parish-warden. A low, drunken, unprincipled lawyer, who had represented himself as a person connected with the aristocracy, very influential, with large expectations, began to interest himself about the parish charities; and nothing is so popular in a parish as doubts whether these charities go to the right persons. By corrupting the churchwardens and overseers and a few others he was appointed legal adviser to the parish. Everything was litigated, and his bills were cheerfully paid, and the man who questioned

them was threatened with a writ. Some of them
were of the most shameful character, such as
removals, making out summonses, advising as
to rates, appearing before the magistrate to
excuse certain defaulters. At last a few began
to rebel; these he threatened with writs.   He
used to attend the vestry meetings half drunk
with a horsewhip, and it was left to me to
fight him. I knew he was a scoundrel, and
I was not afraid of him. I was at first in a
minority, and could do nothing until I changed
the minority into a majority, which I did at
the next election, and which you can always
do if you are in the right and will work for it.
When he knew how the election was going
he rushed into the room with five or six others
and tried to take possession of the ballot-box,
but they failed. He said, "That fellow,"
pointing to me, "has turned the parish against
me by lying, and before I have done with him
he and his children shall come to my house
and beg a piece of bread."

I resolved to have my revenge. It is better
to have a thief for your enemy than for a
friend. The late Board of Churchwardens

and Overseers had to procure a piece of land for a cemetery. Their legal adviser ran up a bill of upwards of seven hundred pounds, which was paid at a public-house the night before they went out of office. This bill was the most extraordinary piece of parish robbery ever known. Charges for supplying ten copies of the agreement, to superintending the drains, to meeting the inspector, to advising as to suitability of the soil. At the foot of this bill was written, "I have examined this bill. —W. ANDERSON." And this was represented as a taxation. I felt this was a robbery, but my colleagues were not disposed to take any steps. We had got rid of him, and why trouble further. But as long as he was in the parish there was danger. I suggested a meeting of the ratepayers, but this was not thought desirable because there was still a strong party in the parish who had profited in various ways by his companionship. At last I managed to have the bill referred to a well-known parish lawyer, who advised us to obtain an order for the taxation of the bill. The Vice-Chancellor hesitated because the bill was paid, but we obtained the order. The lawyer said, as he left the court, "You can't get butter out of a dog's mouth," and more than half the charges were taxed off. Then an order was made for payment of upwards of three hundred pounds. He had previously sold his furniture and moved into another county and then there was further delay. Then he moved a long distance away, where he lived in grand style for a few months. Some of his old companions used to visit him. I was determined to hunt him down for his insults, and, contrary to the advice of the lawyer and the Board, I put an advertisement in the *Telegraph* asking for information as to his whereabouts. As soon as the advertisement appeared his house was besieged with tradesmen from a near town who wanted their money. He returned to the neighbourhood of London, when by accident a friend who had heard me speak of him gave information as to his whereabouts, and in a few days he was in prison, and there I left him. The parish thought I had done a greater service in ridding it of their legal adviser than in saving the common, and I was presented with a service of plate. All this was going on during the common agitation, and it was he who had frightened Wrigsby and told him to tell the court all I had said to him. Plausible in his manner, with a pleasant smile, those who knew but little of his inner character thought him a nice kind gentleman and wondered why I should be so spiteful. I had not forgotten his threat—that was why I followed him.

I then had a little unpleasant business with persons who claimed a right to freehold pews in the parish church. On the appointment of a new vicar these, with other abuses, were swept away. The living, returned at £400 a year, was in the gift of the lord of the manor; but as the Crown made former vicars into bishops, the patron had not for upwards of a century been able to exercise his patronage. He was most anxious to appoint a good man —broad, generous, and charitable, and a strong temperance reformer. As churchwarden I was present at his induction by Bishop Wilberforce, and my colleague said to me, " This is the beginning of a new church history in the parish." A few Sundays after I was standing under the portico of the church looking on the Thames, when a cab drove up with the lord of the manor. He asked, "Is the vicar here?" I replied, "No, my lord, he is preaching this morning at the little iron church on the common." He inquired the way, and how far it was. "I shall be pleased to accompany your lordship." We talked about his appointment of the vicar, which had so far given great satisfaction. I took the opportunity of saying, "During the unpleasantness about the common I was not actuated by any ill-feeling towards your lordship, and if I said anything which in calmer moments I should not have said, I hope your lordship will accept my humble apology. I believe your agent often misrepresented me to your lordship." He replied, "I can quite understand your action in the matter, it is now all over. I am satisfied, and I hope the parishes concerned are satisfied. The best thing for all of us is to forget the past. Here we are." His lordship looked round on cinder heaps and coal-heaps, and inquired, "Is this the common there has been so much trouble about?" "A part of it, my lord." He shook hands, entered the little iron church, and I returned to the parish church in time to hold the plate. To show this reconciliation was not a mere formality, a few years after, when my eldest son left Oxford, he gave him an appointment; and so ended an agitation which originated in weakness but ended in victory. If, when the two gravel diggers came to complain about their potatoes, I could have foreseen what was before me, I should never have written a letter to the newspapers.

The remainder of my story I leave for the present, content to be like him who

" Left half told
The story of Cambuscan bold."

FINIS.

23